Attacked by toy soldiers?

The Vietnam Footlocker was rocking, making the brown paper beneath it rattle. It suddenly overbalanced and fell to the carpet with a soft thud, landing on one end. The hinged top opened a crack of perhaps two inches.

Tiny foot soldiers, about an inch and a half tall, began to crawl out. Renshaw watched them, unblinking. His mind made no effort to cope with the real or unreal aspect of what he was seeing—only with the possible consequences for his survival.

The soldiers were wearing miniscule army fatigues, helmets, and field packs. Tiny carbines were slung across their shoulders. Two of them looked briefly across the room at Renshaw. Their eyes, no bigger than pencil points, glittered.

He threw the pillow. It struck them, knocking them sprawling, then hit the box and knocked it wide open. Insectlike, with a faint, high, whirring noise like chiggers, a cloud of miniature helicopters, painted jungle green, rose out of the box.

—from *Battleground*, by Stephen King

THESE PUFFIN BOOKS WILL REALLY CHILL YOU!

DEATH WALKS TONIGHT

Horrifying Stories

SELECTED BY ANTHONY HOROWITZ

PUFFIN BOOKS

PUFFIN BOOKS
Published by the Penguin Group
Penguin Books USA Inc., 375 Hudson Street, New York, New York 10014, U.S.A.
Penguin Books Ltd, 27 Wrights Lane, London W8 5TZ, England
Penguin Books Australia Ltd, Ringwood, Victoria, Australia
Penguin Books Canada Ltd, 10 Alcorn Avenue, Toronto, Ontario, Canada M4V 3B2
Penguin Books (N.Z.) Ltd, 182-190 Wairau Road, Auckland 10, New Zealand

Penguin Books Ltd, Registered Offices: Harmondsworth, Middlesex, England

First published in Great Britian as
The Puffin Book of Horror Stories by
Penguin Books Ltd., 1994
Published in Puffin Books, 1996

1 3 5 7 9 10 8 6 4 2

Contents

Preface

I was more than surprised when Herbert Small, a senior editor at Puffin, rang me to ask if I'd like to put together this new anthology of horror stories. First of all, I wasn't sure that I actually knew very much about horror. But also it had only been a few months since Herbert had been involved in an unfortunate accident with two articulated lorries and I hadn't realized he was even out of hospital – let alone well enough to work.

When we met at a café near Puffin's London office, he was certainly very pale and I found it hard to avoid staring at the scars on his face and the awful colour of his hands where they poked through the bandages. But he quickly dismissed the accident – 'These things happen' – and we got down to business.

'So what sort of stories are we going to put in this book?' I asked.

Herbert lit a cigarette. 'It's very difficult,' he said.

'On the one hand, young people seem to like really gruesome, bloody stories. The more horrible the better. But then again, most adults – their parents, for example – would rather see them reading a decent classic: *Alice in Wonderland* or Enid Blyton – anything rather than horror.'

'They ought to be grateful to see children reading anything at all,' I said. I had just read a report that put reading in third place behind computer games and television when children were asked what they liked doing most.

Herbert nodded and exhaled cigarette smoke. Rather upsettingly, he exhaled it through the side of his neck and I found myself wondering just how bad his injuries were. 'You may be right,' he said. 'But I don't want a collection that exploits children. You know what I mean. Lurid cover. Silver letters and dripping blood. But just rubbish inside.'

'And I don't want a collection that disappoints the reader,' I replied. 'If it says horror it's got to mean horror. I want stories that bite.'

We talked a little more and agreed to meet three weeks later. I suggested a Wednesday morning at the Puffin offices. To my surprise, however, the editor preferred to meet at night – and at Kensington Cemetery. 'I feel more at home there,' he said.

For the next three weeks I trawled through hundreds of stories. I encountered werewolves, vampires, devils, ghosts, goblins and ghouls. I read about people who had been buried alive and people who had been eaten alive (and couldn't imagine which must have been worse).

And this was my problem.

Real horror is very rare in children's fiction. Take a look in books like *The Oxford Companion to Children's Literature*. Horror stories don't even get a listing. Yes, there are ghost stories. There are plenty of mildly disturbing stories. But if you're looking for a real shudder and perhaps a sleepless night you're basically in the wrong department. Is this really surprising? What sort of adult would want to terrify children?

I met Herbert as agreed in Kensington Cemetery at three o'clock in the morning. He was looking even worse than when I had last seen him. He seemed to have mislaid one ear and part of his chin. His hair was grey and straggly and one of his eyes had locked at an odd angle. Naturally, I was too polite to mention any of this but he must have seen the dismay in my face because he smiled very crookedly (he was also missing several teeth) and told me he had just been at an unusually tough editorial conference at Puffin and hadn't had a chance 'to put myself together'.

'So what have you found?' he asked, perching himself on a gravestone.

'Well,' I began. 'If you really want a horror collection I think we're going to have to look at adult authors. Roald Dahl, for example . . .'

'But he wrote for children.'

'Yes, but he saved his real horror for his adult short stories.' I held up a hand. 'Don't worry,' I said.

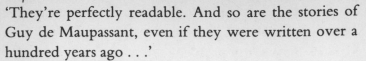

'They're perfectly readable. And so are the stories of Guy de Maupassant, even if they were written over a hundred years ago . . .'

'But they're in French!'

'Don't worry. I'll translate one.'

Herbert was getting excited now. A strange light had come into his eyes and, indeed, into his skin. 'Could you include a bit of *Dracula*?' he asked. 'I'm very fond of stories about people who return from the grave . . .'

'All right,' I said. I wasn't sure about extracts but this was probably the most famous horror story ever written. 'We must also include Stephen King,' I went on. 'He is after all the greatest – and the most successful – living horror writer.'

'But we must have some children's authors,' Herbert insisted. A worm slid out of one of his ears and disappeared behind his spectacles.

I pretended I hadn't seen it. 'Of course,' I said. 'And I have found some brave writers who write what they want to write and don't seem to mind how scary their stories are. Pete Johnson, for example. And Laurence Staig, John Gordon and Robert Westall . . .'

'What about the younger readers?' Herbert asked.

'I've found a story called "The Werewolf Mask". We can put it somewhere in the middle.'

Herbert clapped his hands together. The sound was like an old bone breaking. 'You must write a story too,' he said.

'I shall write a particularly horrible story,' I

promised. I shivered. Meeting in a cemetery might have been fine for atmosphere but it had begun to rain and I was soaked. I wondered why he didn't seem to have noticed.

Herbert stood up. 'All right,' he said. 'But the parents may not like it.'

'As long as the stories are all well written,' I replied, 'they shouldn't have any reason to complain.'

Herbert nodded and limped off into the darkness. And it was very strange because as he disappeared I could have sworn that he . . . well, disappeared. The further away he went the more transparent he became. Then a shaft of moonlight flickered through the trees and he was gone.

I delivered the collection that you now hold about six months later but by then Herbert had left Puffin. It was very odd.

'When did you meet Mr Small?' the new editor asked.

I told her the date.

'But that's imposs . . .' The new editor went very white and hurried out of the room. I never saw her again either.

But at least they published the collection.

I hope Herbert enjoys it. Wherever he may be.

Anthony Horowitz

October 1993

Secret Terror

Pete Johnson

I've never met you but I know this about you: you're terrified of something. It's no use denying it. Everyone is. My mum, for instance, is terrified of intruders. That's why our doors are decorated with a whole variety of locks and chains. There's even a peephole so you can stare at whoever's out there, undetected.

But no lock can stop the intruder I fear. This intruder comes and goes as it pleases. And when it moves, no boards creak under its tread. There's not even the whisper of a sound to alert you where it is.

I can't remember a time when I didn't fear it. But then I was always a very nervous girl. Especially in those years before I went to school. For no one had realized then how short-sighted I was, nor that I was living in a world which was permanently out of focus. It was as if everything was being reflected through one of those distorting mirrors, the ones which twist you into something hideous.

My eyes were as crazy as those mirrors and as treacherous. And then, when I was four, I was suddenly left alone in the house. Mum had been rowing with Dad on the phone (a strange, whispered row) and then she'd rushed out saying, 'I'll only be a minute.'

But she was gone for much longer than that. And I sat in the lounge, cold and tired and afraid. What if Mum didn't come back? What if no one came back? Then I saw something new in the room: a small dark shape, blurred and mysterious. And then, the dark shape ran across the room.

I don't think I'll ever forget the speed with which it ran or its sudden, jerky movements. And before I knew what was happening it was on me, crawling over my feet. I screamed even though the house was empty. And finally my screams were so piercing a neighbour charged in through the back door. Then my mum returned and, a bit later, the doctor came too, because I couldn't stop shivering. He said I was in a state of shock. Well, why wouldn't I be? A lump of dust had turned into a spider.

That was how I overcame all my objections to wearing glasses. I had to know if lurking in the darkest shadows was another spider. At least, armed with my glasses, I could now identify my enemy.

Except when I was in bed at night. One time I saw a spider climbing across my bedroom ceiling. At once I called for my mum. She couldn't see it and said I was letting my imagination run away with me. But she didn't look for very long. And afterwards I thought, what if the spider is still somewhere in my room, nicely camouflaged for now, but later . . . later when I'm asleep it could scurry out of the darkness and continue its climb and perhaps even drop off the ceiling – spiders often do that – and on to my bed. And I'd never know. I'd only feel it as it crawled up my neck and on to my face. To wake up and feel its spindly legs scuttling over your face – I can't think of a worse terror.

I remember one evening when I was watching a James Bond film round at a friend's house: the one where a tarantula crawls over Bond and he has to just lie there, sweating like crazy, until the thing moves off him. And I was horror-struck, not at the prospect of the tarantula biting him, but because he had to stay completely still while a giant spider crawled over him.

I just ran out of the house. My friend's mum rang home and unfortunately, my new stepfather answered. And after hearing about this incident, my vile stepfather decided he'd prove to me that spiders can't do any harm. So one evening, just as I was finishing drying the dishes, he suddenly yelled, 'Catch, Clare,' and threw a spider right at me. Even now I can taste the utter panic and terror I felt then. My mum said the spider had never actually landed on me but no one was really sure where it went. It seemed to just disappear. For days, weeks afterwards I'd wake up convinced the spider was still somewhere on my body.

Happily my stepfather left us shortly afterwards and was replaced later by a stepfather I call Roger, who, whenever I sighted a spider, understood that he had to search properly for it everywhere. No, both he and my mum were very sympathetic. Although occasionally I could see them looking at me questioningly. And I knew they were wondering, is she just putting all this on to gain attention? But something, perhaps something in my eyes, always stopped them accusing me of faking.

As I got older, into my teens, my fear of spiders remained. Only now my reaction to the spiders scared me almost as much as the spiders themselves. For I couldn't seem able to control this fear. And I did try.

I sat down and tried to analyse what it was about spiders I hated so much. Was it their very thin legs or squelchy bodies? Or the fact that they were boneless? (I sometimes wonder how I know all this when I've never got that near to one, nor can even bear to look at one.) For some unknown reason it seems to be only spiders that inspire such blind terror in me.

More recently, some friends tried a kind of aversion therapy on me. They kept emphasizing the positive side of spiders. They told me how good spiders were at catching flies, for instance. And flies spread diseases, unlike spiders. So really, spiders are protecting us from diseases.

Someone even tried to make me feel sorry for spiders. 'Think,' she said. 'That spider you killed was probably a parent and now his poor baby spiders are fatherless or motherless. Next time you see a spider, think of its children.'

But I knew I could no more think of a spider as a parent, than I could an evil spirit. Yet I pretended to go along with it, for I was becoming more and more ashamed of my fear. And although no one ever said anything, I knew what they were thinking: fancy being scared of spiders at her age! And the fact that this fear never left me made it more and more sinister. Was there some deep, dark reason for it? Freud would probably say it pointed to some kind of sexual hang-up. Or perhaps I was just plain neurotic.

Besides, being scared of spiders was such a girly thing. And I am, I suppose, a semi-feminist. I've certainly always despised women who jump on tables and chairs and scream loudly if they see a mouse. Yet, to other people, I must seem as moronic. That's why I tried to bury my fear away. I stopped talking about it and oddly enough I stopped seeing spiders, too. So everyone gradually forgot about it. Even my mum assumed it had vanished away as childhood fears often do.

Then one evening, shortly after my sixteenth birthday, my mum and Roger went out to a dinner-dance. And they were staying at the hotel overnight so they could both drink and make merry (though they never told me that was the reason). I'd originally planned to have some friends visit but I was still getting over flu, so I said I'd just have a bath and an early night instead.

My mum left me a list of instructions headed by, 'Lock yourself in and keep the chain on the door'. And before I took my bath I did just that, even checking the locks on the windows. There's something about being in the bath that makes you feel especially vulnerable, isn't there?

Then I went upstairs. I was already a bit drowsy and my head felt heavy. I decided I'd only have a quick bath tonight. But first I'd lie down on my bed for a minute.

When I woke up the room was covered in darkness. It was two o'clock. I'd slept for nearly four hours. And now it felt all stuffy. I had this full throbbing pain in my head. I bet I wouldn't get off to sleep again for ages. So I decided the best thing would be to have my bath now. I wouldn't stay in the bath long, just long enough for that lovely, tired feeling baths always give me to soak in.

I put on my robe, went into the bathroom, switched on the light and put on the wall heater. The bathroom window's made of pebbled glass, so all I could see was the night's darkness, transformed into something strange and distorted. But I could also hear the rain pattering against the glass and the wind whistling tunelessly. A cold, unfriendly night. A night to sleep through.

I bent down just to test the water was hot enough; I hate lukewarm baths. I stretched my hand out and then shrank back in terror.

I'd almost touched it. If I'd put my hand down just

a couple of centimetres more I would have touched it. I would have touched the largest black spider I'd ever seen.

For a moment I stood completely still, numb with disbelief. I hadn't seen a spider for months, years. I'd assumed they'd disappeared from my life now, and their terror couldn't reach me any more. For I was sixteen, an adult. But as I backed out of the bathroom and into my bedroom I felt myself dwindling away into a small, terrified girl again. Had I really just seen a spider? Or was my flu making me hallucinate? For that spider was so huge it could only have jumped out of one of my nightmares. For years it had hidden itself in the darkest corners of my mind just waiting to come back, stronger than ever, to possess me.

No. Stop. I had to try and be rational about this. Just how had the spider got into the bath? I'd always assumed its only way into the bath was through the drainpipe. That's why every morning I'd check the plug was in the bath. I did it without thinking, a kind of reflex act, like locking the front door after you. So it can't have got in that way.

Well then, it must have just dropped into the bath from the window ledge. Unless – I suddenly remembered Mum had had a bath just before she went out. And I'm sure she left a towel hanging over the edge of the bath, something I would never ever do.

Any second it could climb out of that bath again, down the towel and start running – where? Any second it could scuttle under the bathroom door and into my bedroom. Any second. And there was nothing I could do. Unless I got someone to kill it.

I scrambled into my jeans, then immediately hurled them off again. A spider could be lying somewhere in there. They often crawl into clothes. I shook the jeans hard. Then I got dressed again and rushed downstairs. My plan was to charge into the street and call for help. But even as I stared at the chains I heard Mum's voice, 'The world's full of murderers and rapists,' and saw the newspaper articles she was always showing me of girls attacked at night. I swayed backwards.

For a moment I felt as if I was going to pass out. Flu docs that to you. It creeps back on you again when you're least expecting it. No, I couldn't go out there. But I could ring someone for help, couldn't I? Like Alison, my best friend. She'd understand. She knows how much I fear spiders. Well, she did.

Her phone rang for ages and I was about to put it down when I heard her mother say, 'Yes?'

'Hello,' I said. I didn't know how to begin.

'Who is this? You've woken the whole house up.' Her voice was ice, a block of ice. And I knew I couldn't explain anything to that voice.

However, talking to a voice several degrees below freezing did help me in a way. For as I clicked the phone down, I suddenly had an idea. Something I could do alone. And for the first time that evening I even released a grim smile.

The terror was still there. But I was struggling to the surface of it now. I marched back upstairs and I stood outside the bathroom door. Then I thought, what if the spider's not in the bath any more? What if it's . . . I swatted these fears away. There was a good chance the spider was still in the bath. After all, spiders can sit motionless in the same spot for hours. And if it wasn't in the bath any more — well, at least I'd know.

I banged open the bathroom door, the way Mum did years ago when she thought she heard intruders downstairs. And I was about to switch the light on — when I remembered what a mistake that could be. Insects are drawn to the light. And I didn't want the spider suddenly to start moving about. Not now.

I crept towards the bath. It was pitch dark in there, just as if the whole room was held beneath the spider's shadow. And there it was, so nearly camou-flaged beneath its giant shadow and so completely still that you'd never know it was there. But I knew. I could almost hear it breathing.

Yet, soon, very soon, this spider will terrify me no longer.

First, I slowly and carefully took the towel off the bath. Next, I switched the hot-water tap full on. The water gushed out fiercely, quickly filling the bath. And all of a sudden the spider was moving. It was trying to scramble out of the bath. Almost instinc-tively I backed away. But the water was too fast for it. It could only bob along on the side of the bath. And then it started shrinking into a ball, until finally it looked exactly like what I'd first mistaken it for all those years ago – a large speck of dust. It was disappearing now, becoming smaller and smaller. I edged closer to the bath. Were its legs falling off? I think they were. There were little black specks in the bath now, anyway. Afterwards I really would have to clean that bath out.

I turned away. Now I could almost smell the spider's decomposing body. There was a horrible dank smell in here, just as if I were in an old case full of rotting . . . I turned back. I didn't need to look at the spider now. It would be no more than a black speck. I unplugged the water. And now the water will carry it away for ever. I listened to the water gurgling out. Tonight it seemed a friendly, reassuring sound reminding me of bathtimes with warm radiators and Mum calling, 'Now dry yourself properly. You'll get rheumatism if you rush your drying.' How safe I felt then. If only I could go back. If only I wasn't awake now.

I darted a glance at the spider, then I gaped in disbelief. The spider was moving. It started unfurling itself like a tiny ball of wool, growing bigger and bigger. It hadn't drowned at all. Once again it had cheated me. Once again it had won.

It was scuttling about in the bath now, quickly, and confidently, while I raced around the bathroom too, desperately trying to think what to do next. My head felt hot and throbbing. I should be in bed, resting. But how can I rest when this thing is roaming about the house? I looked at my watch. Only half-past two. Hours and hours yet before morning. Oh, what could I do?

Suddenly I charged downstairs. I had one last desperate plan. I ran into the kitchen and filled two jugs so full of water I spilt half on the way up the stairs again.

I picked up my first jug and let the water tumble out behind the spider. My idea was that the force of the water would push the spider down the plug hole. And it worked. Partly. The water carried the spider about half-way down the bath. So straightaway I poured the second jugful behind the spider, which was by now tightly curled up in a ball. And the water forced it right up to the hole. One more jugful should send it hurtling down the plug hole.

But then I remembered something. In a lot of drains there's a little ledge where spiders sit waiting to come back again. I imagined that spider unfurling itself and then sneaking back into the bathroom again. Once more I started shaking but this time more with anger. I didn't want this fear any more. But I couldn't lose it. Perhaps I'd never lose it.

Yes, I could. Suddenly I flung open the bathroom window, pulled off about half a metre of loo paper and scooped up the spider. I did all this in about ten seconds flat, moving as if I'd been pushed into the wrong speed.

'Hold in there,' I said to myself. 'All you have to do now is throw the thing out of the window.' I took careful aim, holding the paper right by my ear, as I'm not a very good shot, while furiously crunching the paper tighter and tighter. Then I hurled the loo paper right out of the window and watched it plunge on to the back garden like some deformed kite. Tomorrow, no doubt, my stepdad would want to know why there was a roll of toilet paper on the back garden. I found myself smiling. Who cared about that! I was free of it at last. I was free. I even started feeling a bit proud of myself.

Soon I was too exhausted to stay awake very long. I crashed out on the top of my bed and immediately I was asleep and dreaming of a dead bird. I had seen it one morning on the road, lying there all shrivelled up. But that was years ago. I was at primary school. Yet, here it was again. Did nothing ever get lost?

And then I saw something crawling out of the bird's eye . . .

It was such a relief to wake up, even though I was sweating like crazy and I had this strange tickling sensation in my hair.

I was still half asleep, wasn't I, tasting the last moments of my nightmare? How could anything be in my hair? Unless . . . An image flashed through my mind of me holding the loo roll just under my ear, close enough for something to spring on to my face and . . .

And I started to scream. And soon I heard people hammering on the front door calling my name, just like they had all those years before. Only this time they'd never be able to get in. This time no one can help me.

And then I felt a strange tickling sensation creeping down my face.

Battleground

STEPHEN KING

'Mr Renshaw?'

The desk clerk's voice caught him half-way to the elevator, and Renshaw turned back impatiently, shifting his flight bag from one hand to the other. The envelope in his coat pocket, stuffed with twenties and fifties, crackled heavily. The job had gone well and the pay had been excellent – even after the Organization's 15 per cent finder's fee had been skimmed off the top. Now all he wanted was a hot shower and a gin and tonic and sleep.

'What is it?'

'Package, sir. Would you sign the slip?'

Renshaw signed and looked thoughtfully at the rectangular package. His name and the building's address were written on the gummed label in a spiky backhand script that seemed familiar. He rocked the package on the imitation-marble surface of the desk, and something clanked faintly inside.

'Should I have that sent up, Mr Renshaw?'

'No, I've got it.' It was about eighteen inches on a side and fitted clumsily under his arm. He put it on the plush carpet that covered the elevator floor and twisted his key in the penthouse slot above the regular rack of buttons. The car rose smoothly and silently. He closed his eyes and let the job replay itself on the dark screen of his mind.

First, as always, a call from Cal Bates: 'You available, Johnny?'

He was available twice a year, minimum fee $10,000. He was very good, very reliable, but what his customers really paid for was the infallible predator's talent. John Renshaw was a human hawk, constructed by both genetics and environment to do two things superbly: kill and survive.

After Bates's call, a buff-coloured envelope appeared in Renshaw's box. A name, an address, a photograph. All committed to memory; then down the garbage disposal with the ashes of envelope and contents.

This time the face had been that of a sallow Miami businessman named Hans Morris, founder and owner of the Morris Toy Company. Someone had wanted Morris out of the way and had gone to the Organization. The Organization, in the person of Calvin Bates, had talked to John Renshaw. *Pow*. Mourners please omit flowers.

The doors slid open, he picked up his package and stepped out. He unlocked the suite and stepped in. At this time of day, just after 3 p.m., the spacious living-room was splashed with April sunshine. He paused for a moment, enjoying it, then put the package on the end table by the door and loosened his tie. He dropped the envelope on top of it and walked over to the terrace.

He pushed open the sliding glass door and stepped out. It was cold, and the wind knifed through his thin topcoat. Yet he paused a moment, looking over the city the way a general might survey a captured country. Traffic crawled beetlelike in the streets. Far away, almost buried in the golden afternoon haze, the Bay Bridge glittered like a madman's mirage. To the east, all but lost behind the downtown high rises, the crammed and dirty tenements with their stainless-steel forests of TV aerials. It was better up here. Better than in the gutters.

He went back inside, slid the door closed, and went into the bathroom for a long, hot shower.

When he sat down forty minutes later to regard his package, drink in hand, the shadows had marched half-way across the wine-coloured carpet and the best of the afternoon was past.

It was a bomb.

Of course it wasn't, but one proceeded as if it were. That was why one had remained upright and taking nourishment while so many others had gone to that great unemployment office in the sky.

If it was a bomb, it was clockless. It sat utterly silent; bland and enigmatic. Plastique was more likely these days, anyway. Less temperamental than the clock-springs manufactured by Westclox and Big Ben.

Renshaw looked at the postmark. Miami, 15 April. Five days ago. So the bomb was not time-set. It would have gone off in the hotel safe in that case.

Miami. Yes. And that spiky backhand writing There had been a framed photograph on the sallow businessman's desk. The photo had been of an even sallower old crone wearing a babushka. The script slanted across the bottom had read: 'Best from your number-one idea girl – Mom.'

What kind of a number-one idea is this, Mom? A do-it-yourself extermination kit?

He regarded the package with complete concentration, not moving, his hands folded. Extraneous questions, such as how Morris's number-one idea girl might have discovered his address, did not occur to him. They were for later, for Cal Bates. Unimportant now.

With a sudden, almost absent move, he took a small celluloid calendar out of his wallet and inserted it deftly under the twine that crisscrossed the brown paper. He slid it under the Scotch tape that held one end flap. The flap came loose, relaxing against the twine.

He paused for a time, observing, then leaned close and sniffed. Cardboard, paper, string. Nothing more. He walked around the box, squatted easily on his haunches, and repeated the process. Twilight was invading his apartment with grey, shadowy fingers.

One of the flaps popped free of the restraining

twine, showing a dull green box beneath. Metal. Hinged. He produced a pocket knife and cut the twine. It fell away, and a few helping prods with the tip of the knife revealed the box.

It was green with black markings, and stencilled on the front in white letters were the words: G I JOE VIETNAM FOOTLOCKER. Below that: 20 Infantrymen, 10 Helicopters, 2 BAR Men, 2 Bazooka Men, 2 Medics, 4 Jeeps. Below that: a flag decal. Below that, in the corner: Morris Toy Company, Miami, Fla.

He reached out to touch it, then withdrew his hand. Something inside the footlocker had moved.

Renshaw stood up, not hurrying, and backed across the room towards the kitchen and the hall. He snapped on the lights.

The Vietnam Footlocker was rocking, making the brown paper beneath it rattle. It suddenly overbalanced and fell to the carpet with a soft thud, landing on one end. The hinged top opened a crack of perhaps two inches.

Tiny foot soldiers, about an inch and a half tall, began to crawl out. Renshaw watched them, unblinking. His mind made no effort to cope with the real or unreal aspect of what he was seeing – only with the possible consequences for his survival.

The soldiers were wearing minuscule army fatigues, helmets, and field packs. Tiny carbines were slung across their shoulders. Two of them looked briefly across the room at Renshaw. Their eyes, no bigger than pencil points, glittered.

Five, ten, twelve, then all twenty. One of them was

gesturing, ordering the others. They lined themselves up along the crack that the fall had produced and began to push. The crack began to widen.

Renshaw picked one of the large pillows off the couch and began to walk towards them. The commanding officer turned and gestured. The others whirled and unslung their carbines. There were tiny, almost delicate popping sounds, and Renshaw felt suddenly as if he had been stung by bees.

He threw the pillow. It struck them, knocking them sprawling, then hit the box and knocked it wide open. Insectlike, with a faint, high whirring noise like chiggers, a cloud of miniature helicopters, painted jungle green, rose out of the box.

Tiny *phut! phut!* sounds reached Renshaw's ears and he saw pinprick-sized muzzle flashes coming from the open copter doors. Needles pricked his belly, his right arm, the side of his neck. He clawed out and got one – sudden pain in his fingers; blood welling. The whirling blades had chopped them to the bone in diagonal scarlet hash marks. The others whirled out of range, circling him like horseflies. The stricken copter thumped to the rug and lay still.

Sudden excruciating pain in his foot made him cry out. One of the foot soldiers was standing on his shoe and bayoneting his ankle. The tiny face looked up, painted and grinning.

Renshaw kicked at it and the tiny body flew across the room to splatter on the wall. It did not leave blood but a viscid purple smear.

There was a tiny, coughing explosion and blinding agony ripped his thigh. One of the bazooka men had come out of the footlocker. A small curl of smoke rose lazily from his weapon. Renshaw looked down at his leg and saw a blackened, smoking hole in his pants the size of a quarter. The flesh beneath was charred.

The little bastard shot me!

He turned and ran into the hall, then into his bedroom. One of the helicopters buzzed past his cheek, blades whirring busily. The small stutter of a BAR. Then it darted away.

The gun beneath his pillow was a .44 Magnum, big enough to put a hole the size of two fists through anything it hit. Renshaw turned, holding the pistol in both hands. He realized coolly that he would be shooting at a moving target not much bigger than a flying light bulb.

Two of the copters whirred in. Sitting on the bed, Renshaw fired once. One of the helicopters exploded into nothingness. That's two, he thought. He drew a bead on the second . . . squeezed the trigger . . .

It jigged! Goddamnit, it jigged!

The helicopter swooped at him in a sudden deadly arc, fore and aft overhead props whirring with blinding speed. Renshaw caught a glimpse of one of the BAR men crouched at the open bay door, firing his weapon in short, deadly bursts, and then he threw himself to the floor and rolled.

My eyes, the bastard was going for my eyes!

He came up on his back at the far wall, the gun held at chest level. But the copter was retreating. It seemed to pause for a moment, and dip in recognition of Renshaw's superior firepower. Then it was gone, back towards the living-room.

Renshaw got up, wincing as his weight came down on the wounded leg. It was bleeding freely. And why not? he thought grimly. It's not everybody who gets hit point-blank with a bazooka shell and lives to tell about it.

So Mom was his number-one idea girl, was she? She was all that and a bit more.

He shook a pillowcase free of the tick and ripped it into a bandage for his leg, then took his shaving mirror from the bureau and went to the hallway door. Kneeling, he shoved it out on to the carpet at an angle and peered in.

They were bivouacking by the footlocker, damned if they weren't. Miniature soldiers ran hither and thither, setting up tents. Jeeps two inches high raced about importantly. A medic was working over the soldier Renshaw had kicked. The remaining eight copters flew in a protective swarm overhead, at coffee-table level.

Suddenly they became aware of the mirror, and three of the foot soldiers dropped to one knee and began firing. Seconds later the mirror shattered in four places. *Okay, okay, then.*

Renshaw went back to the bureau and got the heavy mahogany odds-and-ends box Linda had given him for Christmas. He hefted it once, nodded, and went to the doorway and lunged through. He wound up and fired like a pitcher throwing a fast ball. The box described a swift, true vector and smashed little men like ninepins. One of the jeeps rolled over twice. Renshaw advanced to the doorway of the living room, sighted on one of the sprawling soldiers, and gave it to him.

Several of the others had recovered. Some were kneeling and firing formally. Others had taken cover. Still others had retreated back into the footlocker.

The bee stings began to pepper his legs and torso, but none reached higher than his rib cage. Perhaps the range was too great. It didn't matter; he had no intention of being turned away. This was it.

He missed with his next shot – they were so god-damn small – but the following one sent another soldier into a broken sprawl.

The copters were buzzing towards him ferociously. Now the tiny bullets began to splat into his face, above and below his eyes. He potted the lead copter, then the second. Jagged streaks of pain silvered his vision.

The remaining six split into two retreating wings. His face was wet with blood and he swiped at it with his forearm. He was ready to start firing again when he paused. The soldiers who had retreated inside the footlocker were trundling something out. Something that looked like . . .

There was a blinding sizzle of yellow fire, and a

sudden gout of wood and plaster exploded from the wall to his left.

. . . *a rocket launcher!*

He squeezed off one shot at it, missed, wheeled and ran for the bathroom at the far end of the corridor. He slammed the door and locked it. In the bathroom mirror an Indian was staring back at him with dazed and haunted eyes, a battle-crazed Indian with thin streamers of red paint drawn from holes no bigger than grains of pepper. A ragged flap of skin dangled from one cheek. There was a gouged furrow in his neck.

I'm losing!

He ran a shaking hand through his hair. The front door was cut off. So was the phone and the kitchen extension. They had a god-damn rocket launcher and a direct hit would tear his head off.

Damn it, that wasn't even listed on the box!

He started to draw in a long breath and let it out in a sudden grunt as a fist-sized section of the door blew in with a charred burst of wood. Tiny flames glowed briefly around the ragged edges of the hole, and he saw the brilliant flash as they launched another round. More wood blew inward, scattering burning slivers on the bathroom rug. He stamped them out and two of the copters buzzed angrily through the hole. Minuscule BAR slugs stitched his chest.

With a whining groan of rage he smashed one out of the air barehanded, sustaining a picket fence of deep slashes across his palm. In sudden invention, he slung a heavy bath towel over the other. It fell, writhing, to the floor, and he stamped the life out of it. His breath was coming in hoarse whoops. Blood ran into one eye, hot and stinging, and he wiped it away.

There, goddamnit. There. That'll make them think.

Indeed, it did seem to be making them think. There was no movement for fifteen minutes. Renshaw sat on the edge of the tub, thinking feverishly. There had to be a way out of this blind alley. There *had* to be. If there was only a way to flank them . . .

He suddenly turned and looked at the small window over the tub. There was a way. Of course there was.

His eyes dropped to the can of lighter fluid on top of the medicine cabinet. He was reaching for it when the rustling noise came.

He whirled, bringing the Magnum up . . . but it was only a tiny scrap of paper shoved under the crack of the door. The crack, Renshaw noted grimly, was too narrow for even one of *them* to get through.

There was one tiny word written on the paper: *Surrender.*

Renshaw smiled grimly and put the lighter fluid in his breast pocket. There was a chewed stub of pencil beside it. He scrawled one word on the paper and shoved it back under the door. The word was: NUTS.

There was a sudden blinding barrage of rocket shells, and Renshaw backed away. They arched through the hole in the door and detonated against the pale blue tiles above the towel rack, turning the elegant wall into a pocket lunar landscape. Renshaw threw a hand over his eyes as plaster flew in a hot rain of shrapnel. Burning holes ripped through his shirt and his back was peppered.

When the barrage stopped, Renshaw moved. He climbed on top of the tub and slid the window open. Cold stars looked in at him. It was a narrow window, and a narrow ledge beyond it. But there was no time to think of that.

He boosted himself through, and the cold air slapped his lacerated face and neck like an open hand. He was leaning over the balance point of his hands, staring straight down. Forty storeys down. From this height the street looked no wider than a child's train track. The bright, winking lights of the city glittered madly below him like thrown jewels.

With the deceptive ease of a trained gymnast, Renshaw brought his knees up to rest on the lower edge of the window. If one of those wasp-sized copters flew through that hole in the door now, one shot in the ass would send him straight down, screaming all the way.

None did.

He twisted, thrust one leg out, and one reaching hand grabbed the overhead cornice and held. A moment later he was standing on the ledge outside the window.

Deliberately not thinking of the horrifying drop below his heels, not thinking of what would happen if one of the helicopters buzzed out after him, Renshaw edged towards the corner of the building.

Fifteen feet . . . ten . . . There. He paused, his chest pressed against the wall, hands splayed out on the rough surface. He could feel the lighter fluid in his breast pocket and the reassuring weight of the Magnum jammed in his waistband.

Now to get around the goddamn corner.

Gently, he eased one foot around and slid his weight on to it. Now the right angle was pressed razorlike into his chest and gut. There was a smear of bird guano in front of his eyes on the rough stone. Christ, he thought crazily. I didn't know they could fly this high.

His left foot slipped.

For a weird, timeless moment he tottered over the brink, right arm back watering madly for balance, and then he was clutching the two sides of the building in a lover's embrace, face pressed against the hard corner, breath shuddering in and out of his lungs.

A bit at a time, he slid the other foot around.

Thirty feet away, his own living-room terrace jutted out.

He made his way down to it, breath sliding in and out of his lungs with shallow force. Twice he was forced to stop as sharp gusts of wind tried to pick him off the ledge.

Then he was there, gripping the ornamented iron railings.

He hoisted himself over noiselessly. He had left the

curtains half drawn across the sliding glass partition, and now he peered in cautiously. They were just the way he wanted them – ass to.

Four soldiers and one copter had been left to guard the footlocker. The rest would be outside the bathroom door with the rocket launcher.

Okay. In through the opening like gangbusters. Wipe out the ones by the footlocker, then out the door. Then a quick taxi to the airport. Off to Miami to find Morris's number-one idea girl.

He took off his shirt and ripped a long strip from one sleeve. He dropped the rest to flutter limply by his feet, and bit off the plastic spout on the can of lighter fluid. He stuffed one end of the rag inside, withdrew it, and stuffed the other end in so only a six-inch strip of saturated cotton hung free.

He got out his lighter, took a deep breath, and thumbed the wheel. He tipped it to the cloth and as it sprang alight he rammed open the glass partition and plunged through.

The copter reacted instantly, kamikaze-diving him as he charged across the rug, dripping tiny splatters of liquid fire.

Renshaw straight-armed it, hardly noticing the jolt of pain that ran up his arm as the turning blades chopped his flesh open.

The tiny foot soldiers scattered into the footlocker.

After that, it all happened very rapidly.

Renshaw threw the lighter fluid. The can caught, mushrooming into a licking fireball. The next instant he was reversing, running for the door.

He never knew what hit him.

It was like the thud that a steel safe would make when dropped from a respectable height. Only this thud ran through the entire high-rise apartment building, thrumming in its steel frame like a tuning fork.

The penthouse door blew off its hinges and shattered against the far wall.

A couple who had been walking hand in hand below looked up in time to see a very large white flash, as though a hundred flash-guns had gone off at once.

'Somebody blew a fuse,' the man said. 'I guess – '

'What's that?' his girl asked.

Something was fluttering lazily down towards them; he caught it in one outstretched hand. 'Jesus, some guy's shirt. All full of little holes. Bloody, too.'

'I don't like it,' she said nervously. 'Call a cab, huh, Ralph? We'll have to talk to the cops if something happened up there, and I ain't supposed to be out with you.'

'Sure, yeah.'

He looked around, saw a taxi, and whistled. Its brake lights flared and they ran across to get it.

Behind them, unseen, a tiny scrap of paper floated down and landed near the remains of John Renshaw's shirt. Spiky backhand script read:

Hey, kids! Special in this Vietnam Footlocker!
(For a Limited Time Only)

1 Rocket Launcher
20 Surface-to-Air 'Twister' Missiles
1 Scale-Model Thermonuclear Weapon

The Vacancy

ROBERT WESTALL

It was in a side-street, in the window of a little brown-brick office. Neatly written, on fresh clean card:

> Vacancy available.
> For a bright keen lad.

Martin pulled up, surveyed it suspiciously. Why specify a lad? Illegal, under the Sex-discrimination Act. England was a land of equal opportunity; to be unemployed. Martin laughed, without mirth. The employment-police would be on to that straight away, and he didn't want to get involved with the employment-police. But perhaps the employment-police wouldn't bother coming down here. It was such a dingy lost little street. In all his travels he'd never come across a street so lost.

He parked his bike against the dull brown wall. An

early 1980s racing-bike, his pride and joy. Salvaged from the conveyor-belt to the metal-eater in the nick of time, rusty and wheelless. He'd haunted the metal-eater for months after that, watching for spare parts. The security cameras round the metal-eater watched him; or *seemed* to watch him. They moved constantly, but you could never tell if they were on automatic.

Anyway, he'd rebuilt the bike; resprayed it. Spent three months' unemployment benefit on oil and aerosols. Now it shone, and got him round from district to district. The district gate-police didn't like him wheeling it through, but it wasn't illegal. The government hadn't bothered making bikes illegal, just stopped production altogether, including spare parts. Cycling had imperceptibly died out.

You had to be careful, travelling from district to district. In some, the unemployed threw stones and worse. In others, it was said, they strung up strangers from lamp-posts, as government spies. Though that was probably a rumour spread by the gate-police. He'd never suffered more than the odd, half-hearted stone, even in the beginning. Now, they all knew his bike, gathered round to get the news.

But he'd travelled far that morning, further than ever before, because of the row with his father.

'Your constant moaning makes me sick,' the old man had said, putting on his worker's cap with the numbered brass badge. 'I keep you – you get free sport, free contraceptives, free drugs and a twenty-channel telly. You lie in bed till tea-time. At your age . . .'

'You had a job,' shouted Martin. 'In 1981, at the age of sixteen, you were given a job, which you still have.'

'Some job. Two hours a day. Four times in two hours a bloody bell rings and I check a load of dials and write the numbers in a book that nobody needs and nobody reads. Call that a job for a trained electrician?'

'You have a reason to get up in the morning – mates at work.'

'*Mates?* I see the fore-shift when I clock on, and the back-shift when I clock off. My nearest *mate* is ten minutes' walk away. Where *you* going?'

'Out. On my bike.'

'You think you're so bloody clever wi' that bike. *And* your bloody wanderings. Why can't you stay where you were born, like everybody else?'

''Cos I'm not like everybody else. And *they're* not going to make me.'

'You want to button your lip, talking like that. Or *they'll* hear you.'

'Or *you'll* tell them.' Then Martin saw the look on his father's face and was sorry. The old man would never do a thing like that. Not like some fathers . . .

He was still staring at the card offering the vacancy when a blond kid came out and spat on the pavement with a lot of feeling.

'Been havin' a go?' asked Martin mildly.

'It's a con,' said the kid. 'They set you an intelligence test that would sink the Prime Minister.' He was no slouch or lout, either. Still held himself upright;

switched-on blue eyes. Another lost sixth-former. 'Waste of time!'

'I don't know . . .' said Martin. In school, he'd been rather sharp on intelligence tests.

'Suit yourself,' said the blond kid, and walked away.

Martin still hesitated. Then it started to rain, spattering his thin jeans. That settled it. The grey afternoon looked so pointless that even failing an intelligence test sounded a big thrill. Sometimes they gave you coffee . . .

He walked in; the woman sitting knitting looked up, bored, plump and ginger. Pale blue eyes swam behind her spectacles like timid tropical fish.

'What's the vacancy?'

'Oh . . . just a general vacancy. Want to apply?'

He shrugged. 'Why not?' She passed him a ballpoint and a many-paged green intelligence test.

'Ready?' She clicked a stopwatch into action, and put it on the desk in front of her, as if she'd done it a million times before. 'Forty minutes.' He sighed with satisfaction as his ballpoint sliced into the test. It was like biting a ham sandwich, like coming home.

An hour later, she was pushing back agitated wisps of ginger hair and speaking into the office intercom, her voice a squeak of excitement, a near-mad glint in her blue tropical-fish eyes.

'Mr Boston – I've just tested a young man – a very high score – a very high score indeed. Highest score in *months.*'

'Contain yourself, Miss Feather. What is the score?' It was a deliberately dull voice that not only killed her excitement dead as a falling pigeon, but made her pull down her plaid skirt, already well below her knees.

'Four hundred and ninety-eight, Mr Boston.'

'Might be worth giving him a PA 52. Yes, try him with a PA 52. We've nothing better to do this afternoon.'

PA 52 was twice as thick as the other one. As Martin took it, a little warm shiver trickled down his spine. Gratitude? To *them*? For what? Not rejecting him outright, like the blond kid? He smashed down the gratitude with a heavy metal fist; they'd only fail him further on. They were just playing with him. They had no job; there were no jobs. Still, he might as well get something out of his moment of triumph.

'Could I have a cup of coffee? Before I start?'

'Oh, I think we could manage a cup of coffee. You start, and I'll put it by your elbow when it's ready.' She clucked around him like she was an old mother hen, and he the only egg she'd ever laid. Smoothly, with a sense of ascending power, he began to cut through PA 52.

'Sit down,' said Mr Boston, steepling long nicotined fingers. He consulted PA 52 slyly, slantingly. 'Erm . . . Martin, isn't it?'

'Mmmm,' said Martin. He thought that Boston, with his near-religious air of relaxed guilt and pinstripe brown suit (shiny at cuff and elbow, and no doubt backside, if backside had been visible) was more like a careers officer than any employer. Employers were much better dressed, ran frantic fingers through their hair, and expected to answer the phone any minute. Still, he'd only met two employers in his life; they'd turned him down before he left school.

'I see you're interested in working with people?'

'Oh, yes, *very*,' said Martin, outwardly eager, inwardly mocking. You were taught in first-year always to say you were terribly keen on people. Jobs with machinery no longer existed; only computers talked to computers now.

'I see leadership potential here.' Boston peered into PA 52 like it was a crystal ball. 'A lot of leadership. Do you find it easy to persuade others ... your friends ... to do what *you* want?'

'Oh yes.' Martin thought of the copies of his underground newspaper, rolled up and pushed down the hollow tubes of his bike, ready for distribution to the various districts. Getting the newspaper team together had taken a lot of persuasion. Persuading pretty little girls to be the news-gatherers, which meant sleeping with grubby elderly civil servants for the sake of their pillowtalk. Getting the printers, with their old hand-operated cyclostyling machine, set up in a makeshift hut in the middle of Rubbishtip 379, after the spy-cameras, sprayed daily with salt water, had rusted solid and stood helpless as stuffed birds. 'Yes, I find it easy to persuade others to do what I want.'

'*Good*,' said Mr Boston. He leaned forward to his intercom. 'Miss Feather – bring our friend Martin here another cup of coffee – the continental blend this time, I think.' Somewhere in the small terraced building a large electrical machine began to hum, slightly but not unpleasantly vibrating the old walls. Some percolator, Martin thought, with a slight smile. He was already starting to feel proprietorial, patronizing about this old dump.

Boston re-steepled his fingers, and slantingly consulted PA 52 again. 'And bags of initiative . . . you're a good long way from home, here. Five whole districts. Have you walked? You must be fit.'

'I've got an old bicycle . . .'

'A bike? Bless my soul.' So great was Boston's surprise that he took off his spectacles, folded their arms neatly across each other, and popped them into the breast-pocket of his suit. He surveyed Martin with naked eyes, candid, weary and brown-edged as an old dog's. 'I haven't seen a bike in years, though I did my share of riding as a boy. Where did you find this bike?'

'At the metal-eater. Had to build it up from bits.'

Mr Boston's excitement was now so great that he had to put his spectacles on again. 'Yes, yes, your mechanical aptitude and manual dexterity show up here on PA 52. And your patience. But . . .' and his voice fell like the Tellypreacher's when he came to the Sins of the Flesh, 'it wasn't awfully honest, was it, taking that bike away from the metal-eater? It already belonged to the State . . .'

Martin's heart sank. This was the point where the job interview fell apart. Even before he got his second cup of coffee. It had been going so well . . . but he knew better than to try to paper over the cracks. He hardened his heart and got up.

'Stuff the State,' he said, watching Boston's eyes for the expression of shock that would be the last pay-off of this whole lousy business.

But Boston didn't looked shocked. He took off his spectacles and waved them; a look of boyish glee suffused his face.

'Stuff the State . . . exactly. Well, not exactly . . .' he corrected himself with an effort. 'We all depend upon the State, but we know it isn't omniscient. To the mender of washing-machines, the State supplies split-pins at a reasonable price, within a reasonable time. But suppose our supply of split-pins has run out already, because we imprudently neglected to reorder in time? We still want our split-pins *now* – even if we have to pay twice the legal price. That is my . . . our . . . little business. Greasing the wheels of State, as I always tell my wife (who is a director of our little firm).' He polished his spectacles enthusiastically with a little stained brown cloth, taken from his spectacle-case for the purpose.

'And if we get caught?' asked Martin; but his mood soared.

'A heavy fine . . . the firm will pay. Or a short prison sentence; that soon passes. We're commercial criminals, not political. We do not wish to overthrow the State, only oil its wheels, oil its wheels. The State understands this.'

They eyed each other. Martin still thought Boston didn't talk like a businessman. But the chances this firm offered . . . His own bedsitter, perhaps a firm's van . . . better still, a chance to smuggle on his own behalf. Not just paper for the newspaper . . . perhaps high-grade steel tubing for guns. He looked at Boston doubtfully; jobs just didn't grow on trees like this. Boston licked his lips, almost pleading, like an old spaniel.

'Sounds a good doss,' said Martin doubtfully.

'Then you accept the vacancy? You're a most suitable candidate.'

Miss Feather came in with the second cup of coffee.

'Will there be a chance to travel?' asked Martin.

'Almost immediately,' said Mr Boston, and Miss Feather nodded in smiling agreement. 'We will have to process you now. Would you mind waiting in here?'

The waiting-room was tiny. Just enough room for a bentwood chair, and a toffee-varnished rack containing a few worn copies of the State magazine at the very end of their life. Martin was surprised anybody had ever bothered to read them; everyone knew they were all glossy lies. There was a strange selection of posters on the walls – Fight Tooth Decay, an advert for the local museum of industrial sewing-machines, and a travel poster featuring an unknown tropical island. Martin wondered if his new job would take him anywhere near there. His head was whirling with the strange drunkenness of accepting and being accepted. Blood pounded all over his body. The vibrations of that damned machine were coming through the waiting-room walls, and going right through his head. It sounded a clapped-out machine, as if it was trying but would never make it.

Too late, the tiny size of the waiting-room warned him; the oppressive warmth. He pulled at the closed door, but it had no handle this side. He hammered on it; heavy metal.

Then there was a crack of blue darkness inside his head. When he opened his eyes again, he was standing in a room exactly the same size, but walled with stainless steel and excruciatingly cold. He shivered, but not just with cold.

There was a great round window set in the door. In the window floated the moon, only it was too big, pale blue and green, scarfed in a white that could only be clouds. Below were low white hills like ash-tips. Nearer, lying on the ashy soil, what looked like heaps of the stringy frozen chops you found in the deep-freeze of the most wretched supermarkets. From among the heaps, white skulls watched him, patiently waiting.

But much worse was the black sky, the totally black sky. In which stars glowed huge and incandescent, red, blue, yellow, orange. Some pulsed, at varying rhythms; others shone steadily.

'There!' Boston's voice came from a grille above

the door, crackly with radio-static. 'There's your vacancy, Martin. Outer space. The biggest vacancy there
is!' His voice was almost gentle, almost proud, almost
pleading. 'Look your fill – I can only give you
another minute.'

Quite unable to think of anything else to do, Martin
continued to gaze at the pulsing stars. Then the door
of the capsule slid aside. His body, sucked outwards
by the vacuum, turning slowly in the low gravity,
exploded in half-a-dozen places in rapid succession.
The force of the explosions shot out great clouds of
red vapour that sank swiftly to the surface of the
white ash. Continuing explosions drove his disintegrat-
ing body across the mounds of his predecessors like an
erratic fire-cracker. Then, indistinguishable from the
rest of the heaps, except for its fresh redness, it settled
to the freeze-drying, vacuum-drying of total vacancy.

'It always seems to me a pity,' said Mr Boston, 'that
anything as wonderful as the Moon Teleport should
have been reduced to *this* use. We could have con-
quered space, if we'd only discovered how to bring
people *back*. Now it's no more than a garbage-
disposal unit.'

'I always feel so flat afterwards,' said Miss Feather.
She lifted a faded print of Constable's *Haywain* from
the wall, revealing a row of stainless-steel buttons and
a digital read-out in green.

11,075,019

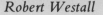

She tapped the buttons rapidly. The number went down one.

11,075,018

Then resumed its inexorable climb.

11,075,019
11,075,021

Miss Feather gave a slight shudder of distaste, and replaced *The Haywain.*

'Pity we can't send them all that way.' She pressed her hairstyle back into place with the aid of her compact-mirror.

'Do you know how much it costs to send *one* to the moon?' asked Boston. 'No, we can only send the dangerous ones. The ones that qualify for the vacancy.'

'*Was* he dangerous?'

'He might have become so. Intelligence, leadership, initiative, mobility, ingenuity, curiosity – all the warning signs were there. It doesn't pay to be sentimental, Miss Feather – I believe young tiger-cubs are quite cuddleable in their first weeks of life. Nevertheless, they become tigers. We remove the tiger-cubs so that the rest, the sheep, may safely graze, as one might put it. I only fear we might not catch enough tiger-cubs in time. The young keep on coming like an inexorable flood, wanting what their fathers and grandfathers had. They could sweep us away.'

They sat looking at each other, in mildly depressed silence.

'That bicycle was a sure sign,' said Boston at last. 'Most original – first I've seen in years. Originality is always a danger. I'd better get the bike off the street, before it's noticed. Ring the metal-eater people, will you?'

Miss Feather rang; put the kettle on for another cup of coffee. Mr Boston came back empty-handed, perturbed.

'It's gone. Someone's taken it.'

'A sneak-thief?'

'Then he's a very stupid sneak-thief,' said Boston savagely. 'Stealing a unique object he'd never dare ride in public.'

'You don't think one of his friends . . . should we ring for the police?' Her hand went to the necklace round her throat, nervously.

'To report the theft of a bicycle that didn't belong to us in the first place? They'd think that pretty irregular. They'd want to know where our young friend Martin had got to . . .'

'Shall we ring the Ministry?'

'My dear Miss Feather, they'd think we were losing our nerve. You don't fancy premature retirement, do you?'

She paled. He nodded, satisfied. 'Then I think we'd better just sit it out.'

Facing each other with a growing silent unease, as the light faded in the grubby street outside, they settled down to wait.

The Twitch

GUY DE MAUPASSANT

Translated by Anthony Horowitz

The dinner guests strolled into the hotel dining-room and sat down in their places. The waiters served them slowly at first to allow the late-comers time to arrive so that they wouldn't have to go back for more plates. And the older bathers, the regulars who had already been here for much of the season, watched with interest each time the door opened and closed, anxious to see new faces appear.

This is the one big event in a health resort.

We all wait until dinner to size up the new arrivals, to guess who they are, what they do, what they think. A single desire prowls through our imagination. It is the hope of meeting someone, of becoming friendly with them, even perhaps of falling in love. In a world where you're for ever rubbing shoulders with complete strangers, the people next to you take on an extra importance. Your curiosity is awakened, your fellow-feeling is sharpened and your desire to be friendly is hard at work.

In a health spa you form serious, long-lasting relationships faster than just about anywhere else. You see everyone all day long and get to know them very quickly. And each new friendship comes complete with a sense of ease and informality as if you've known each other for years. It's a wonderful feeling to open your heart to someone who seems to be opening theirs to you.

And the gloominess of a health spa, the boredom of so many days that are all the same, ensures that a new friendship is hatched each and every hour.

That evening, like every evening, we were waiting for the arrival of someone new.

Only two people came and they were very strange, a man and a woman; father and daughter. They reminded me, straight away, of characters from Edgar Allen Poe; and yet there was a sort of charm about them, a feeling of sadness. I thought they might be the victims of a bereavement. The man was very tall and thin, slightly bent. His hair was completely white, too white − for his face was still young. And there was something grave both in the way he carried himself and in his character; a grimness you would usually associate with protestants. His daughter, aged twenty-four or twenty-five, was small, as thin as him, very pale, with an appearance that was empty, tired, weighed down. You may have met people like these: too weak to handle the cares and necessities of life, too weak to get on with things, to go out and do the things that have to be done. She was also pretty, this young girl. She had the pale beauty of a ghost. And she ate with terrible slowness as if she was virtually unable to move her arms.

It had to be her who had come here to take the waters.

The two of them happened to sit opposite me, on the other side of the table, and I noticed immediately that the father had a most peculiar nervous twitch.

Each time he wanted to reach out for something, his hand described a snake's tongue, making a crazy zig-zag movement before it managed to get what it wanted. The movement annoyed me so much that after a few moments I turned my head away so that I wouldn't have to see it.

I also noticed that the young woman kept, even as she ate, one glove on her left hand.

After dinner, I went for a walk round the park that was part of the spa. It was very hot, that evening. I was walking up and down a shadowy path, listening to the casino band as it struck up a tune from the top of a hill that overlooked the park.

And then I saw, coming towards me at a slow pace, the father and daughter. I nodded at them, the way you nod at any fellow-guest in a health resort; and the man, suddenly stopping, asked, 'Could you, Monsieur, show us a walk that is as short, easy and as pretty as possible – if you'll excuse my interrupting you.'

I offered to lead them to the little valley where a slender river flows. The valley is deep, a narrow gorge between two rocky and wooded escarpments. They accepted.

And naturally we talked about the virtue of taking the waters.

'My daughter,' he told me, 'has a strange illness – we don't know the cause. She suffers from incomprehensible nervous disorders. Sometimes they think it's her heart, sometimes her liver, sometimes her spinal marrow. Now they say it's her stomach. That's why we're here. Me, I'm more of the opinion that it's her nerves. In any case, it's very sad.'

Suddenly I remembered the violent twitch of his hand and I asked him, 'Couldn't she have inherited her illness from you? Don't you have a nervous condition?'

He replied quietly. 'Me? No – my nerves have always been fine.'

But then, after a pause, he went on. 'Ah! You're referring to the way my hand twitches every time I want to take something? That's the result of a terrible experience I once had. Believe it or not – this young girl was once buried alive!'

I could find nothing to say except an 'Ah!' of surprise and emotion. He went on:

Here is my story. It is very straightforward. Juliette had suffered heart murmurs for some time. We thought her heart was diseased and we were prepared for the worst.

One cold day we found her unconscious, dead. She

had just fallen over in the garden. The doctor said that she was deceased. I stood watch over her for a day and two nights; I placed her myself in her coffin, which I accompanied as far as the cemetery where it was placed in our family tomb. This was in the middle of the countryside, in Lorraine.

I had wanted her to be buried with her jewels, her bracelets, necklaces, rings – all presents she had been given by me – and in her first ball-gown.

You can imagine the state of my heart and soul on returning to my home. I had nothing but her, my wife having died a long time before. I returned alone to my bedroom, half-mad, exhausted, and collapsed into my armchair, my mind empty, without the strength to move. I was nothing more than a framework of misery, trembling, flayed alive. My soul was like an open wound.

My old servant, Prosper, who had helped me place Juliette in her coffin and to prepare her for her last sleep, entered soundlessly and asked, 'Monsieur, do you wish to eat or drink something?'

I shook my head without replying.

'Monsieur is making a mistake,' he tried again. 'Monsieur will make himself ill. Would Monsieur like me to put him to bed?'

I said, 'No. Leave me.'

And he went.

How the hours slid past, I don't know. Oh! What a night! What a night! It was cold; my fire had gone out in the main fireplace and the wind, a winter wind, a frozen wind, a great wind full of ice, knocked against the windows with a sinister, repetitive sound.

How did the hours slide past? I sat there, not sleeping, weighed down, overpowered, my eyes open, my legs stretched out, my body powerless, dead and my spirit filled with despair. Suddenly, the great bell by the front door, the great bell of the entrance hall rang out.

I started so suddenly that the seat cracked beneath me. The sound, slow and heavy, shuddered through the empty house as if through a cave. I turned round to look at the time on the clock. It was two o'clock in the morning. Who would want to visit at that hour?

And then the bell rang out twice more. The servants, no doubt, were too afraid to get up. I took a candle and went down. 'Who is there?' I almost asked.

But then, ashamed of my weakness, I slowly drew back the heavy bolts. My heart was beating. I was afraid. With a sudden movement I opened the door and saw in the shadow a white form standing there a little like a ghost.

I drew back, crippled with fear, stammering, 'Who . . . who . . . who are you?'

A voice replied, 'It is me, Father.'

It was my daughter.

Certainly, I thought I'd gone mad. I was reeling backwards as the phantom advanced; I was moving backwards, making the same gesture with my hand to chase it away that you saw a short while ago; that gesture has never left me.

The ghost continued, 'Don't be afraid, Father. I was not dead. Somebody wanted to steal my rings and cut off one of my fingers. My blood began to flow and it was that that woke me up.'

And I saw that indeed she was covered in blood.

I fell to my knees, suffocating, sobbing, gasping for breath.

Then, when I had collected my thoughts a little – I was so bewildered that I barely understood the terrible good fortune that had come my way – I made her come up to my bedroom, made her sit in my armchair. Then I rang violently for Prosper to get him to relight the fire, prepare a drink, and go for help.

The man entered, saw my daughter, opened his mouth in a spasm of dismay and of horror, then fell over rigid, dead, on his back.

It had been he who had entered the tomb, who had mutilated, then abandoned my child; for he was unable to wipe out the traces of his crime. He hadn't even taken care to replace the lid on the coffin, certain that he would not be suspected by me – I who had always trusted him.

You see, Monsieur, that we are indeed two unhappy people.

He fell silent.

Night had come, wrapping itself around the lonely, sad little valley. A strange sort of fear took hold of me, making me feel close to these strange people; this dead girl back from the grave and this father with his dreadful twitch.

I could find nothing to say. I murmured, 'What a horrible thing . . . !'

Then, after a minute, I added, 'Why don't we go back? It's getting chilly.'

And we returned to the hotel.

Freebies

LAURENCE STAIG

The old one-eyed Chinaman who stood in the market place was giving them away. He wasn't giving them to quite *everyone* though. Just people who took his fancy, and who said nice things about the pile of old junk that he was selling from his stall. The old man appeared to like kids, and was acting up like some weird oriental Santa Claus.

Dad had bought a wok from him, for Mum; it was going to be a Christmas present. I'd have preferred to go to Habitat, then you knew where it'd been, but Dad wanted to be his usual 'grassroots' self and buy the thing from the people who knew, *really knew*, about woks.

Dad really can be a boring old fart sometimes.

I wasn't so sure that Mum would know what to do with the thing anyhow, or whether or not she even wanted one. Her mind would be on other things this year, it being the first one without Grannie.

So I ended up being dragged around Chinatown, in the middle of dirty smelly old Soho, on a busy Saturday afternoon, just to get a piece of authentic Chinese frying pan!

The old Chinaman gave me the creeps. A wrinkled prune of a face, with green teeth in a gap-filled mouth, which gasped hot stale breath when he bent down to whisper in my ear.

'Please take it,' he grinned, 'for you. It is present. For you, how you call it? A freebie. With every twenty wok I sell today, a freebie. Yes, it is good, eh?'

He had to be joking, and what a coincidence.

How'd he know about my little hobby, anyhow?

It didn't matter, I'd got another one for the collection.

I looked at the little black plastic box with the dangling chrome chain. He must have read my mind and I could certainly read Dad's. He just groaned. You see, I had a thing about 'give-aways'. Collected them all the time, out of breakfast cereal packets, from petrol stations when we got petrol, supermarkets, anywhere really.

I just liked them, like little trophies. Freebies, as the man said.

'What is it?' I asked.

'It doesn't matter,' said Dad through clenched teeth, 'it's kind of the gentleman to give us anything at all.'

'It clever key-ring,' said the Chinaman, 'instructions in little panel, where battery go. Batteries not in-cluded. You like? I sell you packet, here. Special price to you of one pound ninety pence.'

A leathery hand unfolded to reveal a packet of digital watch batteries, produced from nowhere like a card in a magician's card trick.

Dad's face twitched. I sniggered.

'Crafty old sod,' I said to myself, 'he's just got Dad to shell out on a couple of batteries that he wasn't expecting to have to buy.'

Dad gave him what he sometimes called one of his 'old-fashioned' looks and pressed two pound coins into the Chinaman's palm.

The hand closed.

The old man wished Dad a happy Christmas, and turned to serve another customer who was interested in a wok set.

We didn't even get the change.

That Chinaman was smarter than he looked.

Dad decided that we should walk to Trafalgar Square and perhaps take a bus or taxi back to Brixton. He still wanted to poke around in a few shops, just in case he saw something else he fancied.

'We've got to help Mary through Christmas now that Edith won't be with us this year. You know how dependent she was on the old bat —' he corrected himself, 'the old dear. Help her to take her mind off things, OK?'

He winked at me. I smiled back to keep him happy.

Hypocrite. I knew what he really thought about Grannie.

I hated it, too, when he called Mum Mary, so

familiar, as though I was one of their wally 'drinks party' friends instead of a kid, and I could never get used to Grannie being called by her first name. It wasn't right. As far as I was concerned Grannie was Grannie, and she'd always been around.

'You're growing up now, Sarah,' he'd said to me once, 'you must start to behave more like an adult. I also think it's about time you stopped playing with all those stupid gimmicky toys you litter your room with.'

He always went on and on about how we were slaves of the 'consumer society' as he called it, and how I was a mindless dingbat to go along with it all.

That was a joke coming from a middle-aged bloke who thought he was really IT.

Me? I just liked freebies, that was all.

Dad hated the fact that the old Chinese prune had given me another toy. The joke was on him though: he'd bought me the batteries to go with it!

As we walked down Charing Cross Road I turned the little plastic tag case over in my hand. I wondered at first why a key-ring needed batteries, but then I realized what it was.

In gold lettering on one side was a line of Chinese letters; beneath that in English it simply said 'Chang's Quality Woks, Brewer Street, London, England (main distributors)'.

On the other side of the tag it said 'Key-Finder'.

The little yellow paper stuffed inside the base explained it all in sentences my teacher wouldn't have liked: *Kee-Finder will nether let yuu down if kees yuu lose or mislay. Just whistle. If yor keys are within a 30' radios our tag will immeddiately return call with a serees of clere tones.*

It was one of those lost-key locators. I was really pleased.

I couldn't wait to try it out.

Dad wanted to go into a bookshop near the National Gallery, 'Better Books'. He wanted to get Mum (or Mary) another present. I followed him in while trying to fit the pill-shaped batteries into the base of the key tag.

The shop was jam-packed. Christmas shoppers, cookery books and pictures of the Royal Family everywhere.

A lady in the shop, with glasses and a bun on the back of her hair, pinned a big round yellow badge on my coat lapel. She asked me if I liked books and wished me happy Christmas. There was a miniature book stuck in the centre of the badge, the size of a postage stamp. It opened, with pages like a real book. Above this was the message: *Better books are Better!*

It was a really good freebie. I hadn't seen one like that before.

Dad took my badge off when he saw it, and slapped it down on the counter. The lady with the bun glared at him.

Dad (or Jim if we're into parent-speak), was getting himself all worked up again. Mumbling about me being an easy target, a sucker for it all.

He bought a hi-fi magazine on the way out of the

shop, and there was a freebie stuck to the cover with a bit of Sellotape. A Hi-fi Casebook pencil sharpener. It was clever. A little plastic compact disc with the sharpener on the other side of the spindle hole. On the way home he never lifted his head out of his precious hi-fi magazine once! Typical. He's just as much of a consumer-head as everyone else!

He wouldn't let me whistle on the bus, but when we got off at Brixton Hill I tried to get the Key-Finder to work.

So I whistled. I whistled at it, whistled in it, practically took the thing apart. Nothing.

Dad got mad, which was *really* ironic considering all the fuss he'd been making about the thing, said he'd a mind to go all the way back to Soho and give the man his batteries back.

I wasn't *that* bothered. After all, it had been free, it looked pretty and I could still put my keys on it if I wanted to.

But I had another idea, another use for it.

'Are you going to chuck it?' asked Dad as we turned into our drive, past the dustbins.

I shook my head.

Dad stopped and turned on his heels. A single finger was lifted.

I'm warning you, are you listening, young lady? You leave Dylan alone, he's got a hard enough life as it is trying to survive in the Brixton Hill gardens with all that other nonsense you've fixed on the poor little devil's collar!'

I just smiled, politely, and then shoved the key tag deep into my coat pocket. Dad could be *such* a pain.

Dylan was scratching himself on the porch mat as we walked up the path.

The front door opened. Mum (or Mary) stood in the doorway.

She didn't look good. I sighed.

Dad (or Jim) was making caustic comments in the living-room about how the Christmas booze seemed to be prematurely lowering its level. The surface line in the large bottle of Gordon's, which sat on the Habitat trolley, was certainly nearing the bottom.

Even I noticed that.

But then again, Mum was depressed.

I spent my time out in the kitchen trying to make the key tag work, but it wouldn't give out so much as a peep. Dylan had struggled into the kitchen too.

Mum and Dad were rowing again and Dylan wanted to get out of their way.

I didn't blame him.

Dad was making the usual fuss about how she had to pull herself together, she'd a family (and him) to look after, just because Edith's number had come up we didn't have to spend the entire Christmas in mourning.

Then he threatened to re-convert the grannie-flat which we'd had built next to the garden shed. He'd always threatened to make it into an outdoor aquarium.

Ah well.

And my new freebie didn't work.

Dylan purred smugly down at me from the top of the boiler. His head was lowered from the weight of his great collection of Cat Consumables. Mum called him our 'Consumer Kitty'.

I attached the key tag to his collar along with the other freebies:

his Katto-Kipper personalized name disc

plastic Burger King bun

miniature Coca-Cola bottle

Holiday Inn room tag

MHI luggage label

Kellogg's Munchkin Man

and a Dr Who Energizer ring which wrapped around his neck.

That had been a special 'give-away' at the Arndale Shopping Centre in Croydon; he liked that best of all.

Dylan opened his sleepy eyes and stretched his paws and shook his new toy. Then, with a loud miaow, probably a 'thank you', he made for the kitchen door. His freebies crashed into the cat flap on his way out.

In the living-room they were still rowing.

Dad's voice was getting really loud.

Outside came the rumble of an approaching car. I suddenly had a bad feeling.

I heard Mum's glass smash at almost the same time as we heard the screech of brakes out in the front road.

There was an awful short tangled wail. The kind of sound cats make when they scrap. Then silence.

I heard Dad yell, 'Oh my God, no!'

Dad can be *so* dramatic.

Yesterday was miserable: black and solemn.

Dad blamed me. He was really mad. But it was good of him to dig Dylan a nice neat grave out in the back garden.

He kept muttering about how there had been far too much on his collar, and how the whistling key-ring had been the final straw. Just slowed him down, so when he'd run across the street he was an easy target.

Mum told him to shut up, that he'd upset 'the child'.

'The child' indeed. I just ignored her.

We put Dylan in the soft soil where Mum had planted the Hobson's Garden Centre roses, just in front of the grannie-flat.

We buried him with full honours, all his toys intact. I'd wanted the key-ring back, just as a souvenir, but Mum was almost sick when Dad tried to find it. It was like picking a favourite strawberry out of a collapsed flan.

She called me a funny word. I didn't know what it meant, but I didn't like the sound of it at all.

A ghoul?

You *can* go off parents.

Sleep was very difficult that night, in fact everything was a funny blur. The air in my bedroom seemed thick and it was difficult even to breathe.

I opened the dormer window and looked down into the garden.

It was dark and cold, but winter clear outside.

A grey cloud passed over, and the grass in front of the grannie-flat reflected moonglow once more.

The garden shone.

A newly heaped pile of topsoil marked the spot. I had scratched Dylan's name on a coke can, and fixed it in the ground, a temporary tombstone.

The TV offer peacock wind-chime which hung within the window-frame sang softly as a gentle wind got up.

A last goodnight to Dylan.

I shivered and scrambled back to bed.

I must have forgotten to close the window because I remember the sounds well. So bright. Icy sharp.

There was the rustle and flutter of feathers against branches.

A low warbling sound, and then a single hoot.

It was our owl, and he had come to speak to Dylan.

He'd startled me. Through half-closed eyes I watched as the shadows of the branches shimmered across the bedroom wall. Tangling into twisted claws.

Dylan would sit for hours on the window-ledge. The owl came often. Dad said that it was unusual to find a bird like that in Brixton.

Dylan and the owl were friends. But now he'd have to find somebody else.

I pulled the sheet up tight to my neck, eyelids heavy with sleep.

There was a high-pitched whistle outside.

The owl was preparing to fly from the tree.

It shook its feathers and then let out a strange kind of 'hoot'.

And then another . . . it was really scary.

Almost a whistle.

Just after that I heard a strangled muffled growl, far away, from deep beneath the still cold earth.

I sank and sank, down and down, into the softness of dream.

My eyes were not quite closed. Not yet. But I knew.

From the distance the owl cried out once more. I couldn't do a thing. Couldn't even move. I didn't know if I was awake or dreaming.

There was a familiar scratching on the bark of the tree outside my window. A slow and perhaps painful kind of shifting.

The shadows of branch claws trembled across the wall as something pulled itself along a main bough.

There was a shape framed within the window, dead eyes that glowed, and then the soft plop as it dropped from the sill down on to the floor.

I heard a gasp, the momentary 'puff' of the eider-down as though something heavy had landed on the bed.

Outside the branches rustled. Twigs cracked.

I became aware of a gentle repetitive pumping at the bottom of the bed, and then a warm comforting vibration in the small of my back like an electric motor.

I was afraid. At first.

But I'm a big girl now.

Mum was very excited. 'Hysterical,' Dad said. She kept asking him over and over about the white and ginger hairs at the bottom of the bed. He told her not to be so silly and to 'lay off the sauce'.

I think it was the blood that really bothered her. That and the soil-clogged Burger King bun she found next to the pillow.

I can understand why she was so upset, but she's all right now.

What pissed me off most was Dad, saying that I could never bring another freebie into the house again.

I'll do what I want!

Have I got a surprise for them, for Christmas!

I've been practising my whistles, and I've got lots of ideas for using those key-rings now. I went to Brixton and caught the tube, all the way up to Chinatown, and all on my own too. I got a whole bunch of the tags from the old Chinese wok man.

We did a deal. I'd keep quiet about his fiddle with the batteries.

Tonight I'm going to go and see Grannie at the cemetery.

It's just up the road.

Mum misses her so, and it'll serve Dad right.

The key-ring works fine now. Fine.

Best freebie I've ever had.

Man from the South

ROALD DAHL

It was getting on towards six o'clock so I thought I'd buy myself a beer and go out and sit in a deck-chair by the swimming-pool and have a little evening sun.

I went to the bar and got the beer and carried it outside and wandered down the garden towards the pool.

It was a fine garden with lawns and beds of azaleas and tall coconut palms, and the wind was blowing strongly through the tops of the palm trees, making the leaves hiss and crackle as though they were on fire. I could see the clusters of big brown nuts hanging down underneath the leaves.

There were plenty of deck-chairs around the swimming-pool and there were white tables and huge brightly coloured umbrellas and sunburned men and women sitting around in bathing suits. In the pool itself there were three or four girls and about a dozen boys, all splashing about and making a lot of noise and throwing a large rubber ball at one another.

I stood watching them. The girls were English girls from the hotel. The boys I didn't know about, but they sounded American, and I thought they were probably naval cadets who'd come ashore from the US naval training vessel which had arrived in harbour that morning.

I went over and sat down under a yellow umbrella where there were four empty seats, and I poured my beer and settled back comfortably with a cigarette.

It was very pleasant sitting there in the sunshine with beer and cigarette. It was pleasant to sit and watch the bathers splashing about in the green water.

The American sailors were getting on nicely with the English girls. They'd reached the stage where they were diving under the water and tipping them up by their legs.

Just then I noticed a small, oldish man walking briskly around the edge of the pool. He was immaculately dressed in a white suit and he walked very quickly with little bouncing strides, pushing himself high up on to his toes with each step. He had on a large creamy Panama hat, and he came bouncing along the side of the pool, looking at the people and the chairs.

He stopped beside me and smiled, showing two rows of very small, uneven teeth, slightly tarnished. I smiled back.

'Excuse pleess, but may I sit here?'

'Certainly,' I said. 'Go ahead.'

He bobbed around to the back of the chair and

inspected it for safety, then he sat down and crossed his legs. His white buck-skin shoes had little holes punched all over them for ventilation.

'A fine evening,' he said. 'They are all evenings fine here in Jamaica.' I couldn't tell if the accent were Italian or Spanish, but I felt fairly sure he was some sort of a South American. And old too, when you saw him close. Probably around sixty-eight or seventy.

'Yes,' I said. 'It is wonderful here, isn't it.'

'And who, might I ask, are all dese? Dese is no hotel people.' He was pointing at the bathers in the pool.

'I think they're American sailors,' I told him. 'They're Americans who are learning to be sailors.'

'Of course dey are Americans. Who else in de world is going to make as much noise as dat? You are not American no?'

'No,' I said. 'I am not.'

Suddenly one of the American cadets was standing in front of us. He was dripping wet from the pool and one of the English girls was standing there with him.

'Are these chairs taken?' he said.

'No,' I answered.

'Mind if I sit down?'

'Go ahead.'

'Thanks,' he said. He had a towel in his hand and when he sat down he unrolled it and produced a pack of cigarettes and a lighter. He offered the cigarettes to the girl and she refused; then he offered them to me and I took one. The little man said, 'Tank you, no, but I tink I have a cigar.' He pulled out a crocodile case and got himself a cigar, then he produced a knife which had a small scissors in it and he snipped the end off the cigar.

'Here, let me give you a light.' The American boy held up his lighter.

'Dat will not work in dis wind.'

'Sure it'll work. It always works.'

The little man removed his unlighted cigar from his mouth, cocked his head on one side and looked at the boy.

'*All*-ways?' he said slowly.

'Sure, it never fails. Not with me anyway.'

The little man's head was still cocked over on one side and he was still watching the boy. 'Well, well. So you say dis famous lighter it never fails. Iss dat you say?'

'Sure,' the boy said. 'That's right.' He was about nineteen or twenty with a long freckled face and a rather sharp birdlike nose. His chest was not very sunburned and there were freckles there too, and a few wisps of pale-reddish hair. He was holding the lighter in his right hand, ready to flip the wheel. 'It never fails,' he said, smiling now because he was purposely exaggerating his little boast. 'I promise you it never fails.'

'One momint, pleess.' The hand that held the cigar came up high, palm outward, as though it were stopping traffic. 'Now juss one momint.' He had a curiously soft, toneless voice and he kept looking at the boy all the time.

'Shall we not perhaps make a little bet on dat?' He smiled at the boy. 'Shall we not make a little bet on whether your lighter lights?'

'Sure, I'll bet,' the boy said, 'Why not?'

'You like to bet?'

'Sure, I'll always bet.'

The man paused and examined his cigar, and I must say I didn't much like the way he was behaving. It seemed he was already trying to make something out of this, and to embarrass the boy, and at the same time I had the feeling he was relishing a private little secret all his own.

He looked up again at the boy and said slowly, 'I like to bet, too. Why we don't have a good bet on dis ting? A good big bet.'

'Now wait a minute,' the boy said. 'I can't do that. But I'll bet you a quarter. I'll even bet you a dollar, or whatever it is over here – some shillings, I guess.'

The little man waved his hand again. 'Listen to me. Now we have some fun. We make a bet. Den we go up to my room here in de hotel where iss no wind and I bet you you cannot light dis famous lighter of yours ten times running without missing once.'

'I'll bet I can,' the boy said.

'All right. Good. We make a bet, yes?'

'Sure, I'll bet you a buck.'

'No, no. I make you a very good bet. I am rich man and I am sporting man also. Listen to me.

Outside de hotel iss my car. Iss very fine car. American car from your country. Cadillac –'

'Hey, now. Wait a minute.' The boy leaned back in his deck-chair and he laughed. 'I can't put up that sort of property. This is crazy.'

'Not crazy at all. You strike lighter successfully ten times running and Cadillac is yours. You like to have dis Cadillac, yes?'

'Sure, I'd like to have a Cadillac.' The boy was still grinning.

'All right. Fine. We make a bet and I put up my Cadillac.'

'And what do I put up?'

The little man carefully removed the red band from his still unlighted cigar. 'I never ask you, my friend, to bet something you cannot afford. You understand?'

'Then what do I bet?'

'I make it very easy for you, yes?'

'OK. You make it easy.'

'Some small ting you can afford to give away, and if you did happen to lose it you would not feel too bad. Right?'

'Such as what?'

'Such as, perhaps, de little finger on your left hand.'

'My *what*?' The boy stopped grinning.

'Yes. Why not? You win, you take de car. You looss, I take de finger.'

'I don't get it. How d'you mean, you take the finger?'

'I chop it off.'

'Jumping jeepers! That's a crazy bet. I think I'll just make it a dollar.'

The little man leaned back, spread out his hands palms upwards and gave a tiny contemptuous shrug of the shoulders. 'Well, well, well,' he said. 'I do not understand. You say it lights but you will not bet. Den we forget it, yes?'

The boy sat quite still, staring at the bathers in the pool. Then he remembered suddenly he hadn't lighted his cigarette. He put it between his lips, cupped his hands around the lighter and flipped the wheel. The wick lighted and burned with a small, steady, yellow flame and the way he held his hands the wind didn't get to it at all.

'Could I have a light, too?' I said.

'God, I'm sorry, I forgot you didn't have one.'

I held out my hand for the lighter, but he stood up and came over to do it for me.

'Thank you,' I said, and he returned to his seat.

'You having a good time?' I asked.

'Fine,' he answered. 'It's pretty nice here.'

There was a silence then, and I could see that the little man had succeeded in disturbing the boy with his absurd proposal. He was sitting there very still, and it was obvious that a small tension was beginning to build up inside him. Then he started shifting about in his seat, and rubbing his chest, and stroking the back of his neck, and finally he placed both hands on his knees and began tap-tapping with his fingers against the knee-caps. Soon he was tapping with one of his feet as well.

'Now just let me check up on this bet of yours,' he said at last. 'You say we go up to your room and if I make this lighter light ten times running I win a Cadillac. If it misses just once then I forfeit the little finger of my left hand. Is that right?'

'Certainly. Dat is de bet. But I tink you are afraid.'

'What do we do if I lose? Do I have to hold my finger out while you chop it off?'

'Oh, no! Dat would be no good. And you might be tempted to refuse to hold it out. What I should do I should tie one of your hands to de table before we started and I should stand dere with a knife ready to go *chop* de momint your lighter missed.'

'What year is the Cadillac?' the boy asked.

'Excuse. I not understand.'

'What year – how old is the Cadillac?'

'Ah! How old? Yes. It is last year. Quite new car. But I see you are not betting man. Americans never are.'

The boy paused for just a moment and he glanced first at the English girl, then at me. 'Yes,' he said sharply. 'I'll bet you.'

'Good!' The little man clapped his hands together quietly, once. 'Fine,' he said. 'We do it now. And you, sir,' he turned to me, 'you would perhaps be good enough to, what you call it, to – to referee.' He had pale, almost colourless eyes with tiny black pupils.

'Well,' I said. 'I think it's a crazy bet. I don't think I like it very much.'

'Nor do I,' said the English girl. It was the first time she'd spoken. 'I think it's a stupid, ridiculous bet.'

'Are you serious about cutting off this boy's finger if he loses?' I said.

'Certainly I am. Also about giving him Cadillac if he win. Come now. We go to my room.'

He stood up. 'You like to put on some clothes first?' he said.

'No,' the boy answered. 'I'll come like this.' Then he turned to me. 'I'd consider it a favour if you'd come along and referee.'

'All right,' I said. 'I'll come along, but I don't like the bet.'

'You come too,' he said to the girl. 'You come and watch.'

The little man led the way back through the garden to the hotel. He was animated now, and excited, and that seemed to make him bounce up higher than ever on his toes as he walked along.

'I live in annexe,' he said. 'You like to see car first? Iss just here.'

He took us to where we could see the front drive-way of the hotel and he stopped and pointed to a sleek pale-green Cadillac parked close by.

'Dere she iss. De green one. You like?'

'Say, that's a nice car,' the boy said.

'All right. Now we go up and see if you can win her.'

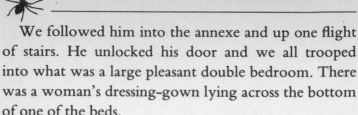

We followed him into the annexe and up one flight
of stairs. He unlocked his door and we all trooped
into what was a large pleasant double bedroom. There
was a woman's dressing-gown lying across the bottom
of one of the beds.

'First,' he said, 'we 'ave a little Martini.'

The drinks were on a small table in the far corner,
all ready to be mixed, and there was a shaker and ice
and plenty of glasses. He began to make the Martini,
but meanwhile he'd rung the bell and now there was
a knock on the door and a coloured maid came in.

'Ah!' he said, putting down the bottle of gin,
taking a wallet from his pocket and pulling out a
pound note. 'You will do something for me now,
pleess.' He gave the maid the pound.

'You keep dat,' he said. 'And now we are going to
play a little game in here and I want you to go off
and find for me two – no tree tings. I want some
nails, I want a hammer, and I want a chopping knife,
a butcher's chopping knife which you can borrow
from de kitchen. You can get, yes?'

'A *chopping knife!*' The maid opened her eyes wide
and clasped her hands in front of her. 'You mean a
real chopping knife?'

'Yes, yes, of course. Come on now, pleess. You can
find dose tings surely for me.'

'Yes, sir, I'll try, sir. Surely I'll try to get them.'
And she went.

The little man handed round the Martinis. We
stood there and sipped them, the boy with the long

freckled face and the pointed nose, bare-bodied except for a pair of faded brown bathing shorts; the English girl, a large-boned fair-haired girl wearing a pale blue bathing suit, who watched the boy over the top of her glass all the time; the little man with the colourless eyes standing there in his immaculate white suit drinking his Martini and looking at the girl in her pale blue bathing dress. I didn't know what to make of it all. The man seemed serious about the bet and he seemed serious about the business of cutting off the finger. But hell, what if the boy lost? Then we'd have to rush him to the hospital in the Cadillac that he hadn't won. That would be a fine thing. Now wouldn't that be a really fine thing? It would be a damn silly unnecessary thing so far as I could see.

'Don't you think this is rather a silly bet?' I said.

'I think it's a fine bet,' the boy answered. He had already downed one large Martini.

'I think it's a stupid, ridiculous bet,' the girl said. 'What'll happen if you lose?'

'It won't matter. Come to think of it, I can't remember ever in my life having had any use for the little finger on my left hand. Here he is.' The boy took hold of the finger. 'Here he is and he hasn't ever done a thing for me yet. So why shouldn't I bet him? I think it's a fine bet.'

The little man smiled and picked up the shaker and refilled our glasses.

'Before we begin,' he said, 'I will present to de – to de referee de key of de car.' He produced a car key from his pocket and gave it to me. 'De papers,' he said, 'de owning papers and insurance are in de pocket of de car.'

Then the coloured maid came in again. In one hand she carried a small chopper, the kind used by butchers for chopping meat bones, and in the other a hammer and a bag of nails.

'Good! You get dem all. Tank you, tank you. Now you can go.' He waited until the maid had closed the door, then he put the implements on one of the beds and said, 'Now we prepare ourselves, yes?' And to the boy, 'Help me, pleess, with dis table. We carry it out a little.'

It was the usual kind of hotel writing desk, just a plain rectangular table about four feet by three with a blotting pad, ink, pens and paper. They carried it out into the room away from the wall, and removed the writing things.

'And now,' he said, 'a chair.' He picked up a chair and placed it beside the table. He was very brisk and very animated, like a person organizing games at a children's party. 'And now de nails. I must put in de nails.' He fetched the nails and he began to hammer them into the top of the table.

We stood there, the boy, the girl, and I, holding Martinis in our hands, watching the little man at work. We watched him hammer two nails into the table, about six inches apart. He didn't hammer them right home; he allowed a small part of each one to stick up. Then he tested them for firmness with his fingers.

Anyone would think the son of a bitch had done this before, I told myself. He never hesitates. Table, nails, hammer, kitchen chopper. He knows exactly what he needs and how to arrange it.

'And now,' he said, 'all we want is some string.' He found some string. 'All right, at last we are ready. Will you pleess to sit here at de table?' he said to the boy.

The boy put his glass away and sat down.

'Now place de left hand between dese two nails. De nails are only so I can tie your hand in place. All right, good. Now I tie your hand secure to de table – so.'

He wound the string around the boy's wrist, then several times around the wide part of the hand, then he fastened it tight to the nails. He made a good job of it and when he'd finished there wasn't any question about the boy being able to draw his hand away. But he could move his fingers.

'Now pleess, clench de fist, all except for de little finger. You must leave de little finger sticking out, lying on de table.'

'*Ex*-cellent! *Ex*-cellent! Now we are ready. Wid your right hand you manipulate de lighter. But one momint, pleess.'

He skipped over to the bed and picked up the chopper. He came back and stood beside the table with the chopper in his hand.

'We are all ready?' he said. 'Mister referee, you must say to begin.'

The English girl was standing there in her pale blue

bathing costume right behind the boy's chair. She was just standing there, not saying anything. The boy was sitting quite still holding the lighter in his right hand, looking at the chopper. The little man was looking at me.

'Are you ready?' I asked the boy.

'I'm ready.'

'And you?' to the little man.

'Quite ready,' he said and he lifted the chopper up in the air and held it there about two feet above the boy's finger, ready to chop. The boy watched it, but he didn't flinch and his mouth didn't move at all. He merely raised his eyebrows and frowned.

'All right,' I said. 'Go ahead.'

The boy said, 'Will you please count aloud the number of times I light it.'

'Yes,' I said. 'I'll do that.'

With his thumb he raised the top of the lighter, and again with the thumb he gave the wheel a sharp flick. The flint sparked and the wick caught fire and burned with a small yellow flame.

'One!' I called.

He didn't blow the flame out; he closed the top of the lighter on it and he waited for perhaps five seconds before opening it again.

He flicked the wheel very strongly and once more there was a small flame burning on the wick.

'Two!'

No one else said anything. The boy kept his eyes on the lighter. The little man held the chopper up in the air and he too was watching the lighter.

'Three!'

'Four!'

'Five!'

'Six!'

'Seven!' Obviously it was one of those lighters that worked. The flint gave a big spark and the wick was the right length. I watched the thumb snapping the top down on to the flame. Then a pause. Then the thumb raising the top once more. This was an all-thumb operation. The thumb did everything. I took a breath, ready to say eight. The thumb flicked the wheel. The flint sparked. The little flame appeared.

'Eight!' I said, and as I said it the door opened. We all turned and we saw a woman standing in the doorway, a small, black-haired woman, rather old, who stood there for about two seconds then rushed forward, shouting, 'Carlos! Carlos!' She grabbed his wrist, took the chopper from him, threw it on the bed, took hold of the little man by the lapels of his white suit and began shaking him very vigorously, talking to him fast and loud and fiercely all the time in some Spanish-sounding language. She shook him so fast you couldn't see him any more. He became a faint, misty, quickly moving outline, like the spokes of a turning wheel.

Then she slowed down and the little man came into view again and she hauled him across the room and pushed him backwards on to one of the beds. He sat on the edge of it blinking his eyes and testing his head to see if it would still turn on his neck.

'I am sorry,' the woman said. 'I am so terribly sorry that this should happen.' She spoke almost perfect English.

'It is too bad,' she went on. 'I suppose it is really my fault. For ten minutes I leave him alone to go and have my hair washed and I come back and he is at it again.' She looked sorry and deeply concerned.

The boy was untying his hand from the table. The English girl and I stood there and said nothing.

'He is a menace,' the woman said. 'Down where we live at home he has taken altogether forty-seven fingers from different people, and he has lost eleven cars. In the end they threatened to have him put away somewhere. That's why I brought him up here.'

'We were only having a little bet,' mumbled the little man from the bed.

'I suppose he bet you a car,' the woman said.

'Yes,' the boy answered. 'A Cadillac.'

'He has no car. It's mine. And that makes it worse,' she said, 'that he should bet you when he has nothing to bet with. I am ashamed and very sorry about it all.' She seemed an awfully nice woman.

'Well,' I said, 'then here's the key of your car.' I put it on the table.

'We were only having a little bet,' mumbled the little man.

'He hasn't anything left to bet with,' the woman said. 'He hasn't a thing in the world. Not a thing. As a matter of fact I myself won it all from him a long while ago. It took time, a lot of time, and it was hard work, but I won it all in the end.' She looked up at the boy and she smiled, a slow sad smile, and she came over and put out a hand to take the key from the table.

I can see it now, that hand of hers; it had only one finger on it, and a thumb.

The Werewolf Mask

KENNETH IRELAND

The mask looked just like a horrible werewolf with blood dripping from its fangs. It was one which fitted right over Peter's head, with spaces for his eyes so that when he looked out the movement gave an extra dimension of horror to the already terrifying expression on the rubber face. The hair hanging down from the top of the mask looked real, as did the hair and whiskers drooping from the sides and face. It was very satisfying, Peter felt, as soon as he had been into the joke shop and bought it.

Something, however, was missing. While the mask seemed realistic enough, it was his hands which were wrong. If a human could really turn into a werewolf, it would not be only the face which would change, but the hands would grow hairy as well. He discovered this when he unwrapped the paper bag in which he had bought it and went upstairs to try the effect in front of his dressing-table mirror. As long as he kept his hands hidden, all was well, but once his hands were seen, they were far too smooth. In fact, they weren't hairy at all. It was rather disappointing, but nevertheless he thought that he'd try out the effect anyway. His mother was in, so making grunting and drooling noises he loped away down the stairs.

He went into the living-room where his mother was darning some socks, flung open the door suddenly and leaped in, arms raised to his shoulders, fingers extended like claws, and growling ferociously.

'My goodness,' said his mother, looking up, 'what on earth made you waste your money on a thing like that?'

'I thought it was rather good,' said Peter, not at all put out. 'Doesn't it look – well, real?'

'Well, it was your birthday money, so I suppose you could spend it how you liked,' said his mother placidly, returning to the socks. 'I don't know how you manage to get such large holes in these, I really don't. I think it must be the way you drag them on.'

'But doesn't it look just like a werewolf?' asked Peter, taking the mask off and examining it carefully.

'It would, I suppose, except there are no such things and never have been such things as werewolves. I think you've wasted your money on something which is of no real use,' his mother replied. 'The money would have been better spent on some new pairs of socks. Still, your Aunty Doreen did tell you to spend it on something to amuse you, so I suppose we can't expect everything.'

'The thing that's wrong with it is my hands,' said Peter. 'The face is all right, but the hands are wrong to go with it, don't you think?'

He put the mask on again and held his hands out for her to see the effect. She glanced at him briefly. 'Putting a mask on like that won't make your hands look different from a boy's,' she said. 'The only thing you could do is wear gloves, your woolly ones perhaps, to disguise them.'

Since she was taking no more notice of him, he went back upstairs, drew a pair of woolly gloves from a drawer in his dressing table, and tried the effect this time. Well, perhaps it wasn't all that bad. At least the gloves gave some kind of appearance of hairiness, but it was still not quite right. He tried combing the backs of the gloves, but that was no good at all. When he tried the claw effect, it was not half as good as when his nails were showing.

He still had some money left, so he went back to the joke shop, taking the mask with him.

'Have you got,' he asked, 'anything like hairy hands?'

The shopkeeper, being a bit of a joker himself, looked down at his hands and asked if they would do. Then he looked down at his feet behind the counter and as if in surprise announced that he hadn't got pigs' trotters, either.

'No, I mean,' explained Peter carefully, 'like I bought this werewolf mask, I wonder if you have a kind of hairy hand mask to go with it. You know, to make the whole thing look – well, more real?'

'Hairy, with sort of claws, you mean?' asked the shopkeeper, nodding. 'I might have. Hang on.'

He went along the shelves behind the counter, opened first one drawer then another, and at the third drawer extracted a transparent plastic bag which he placed on the counter.

'These do?' he asked.

Peter picked them up eagerly, and inspected the contents through the plastic. They looked about right.

'Can I try them on?' he asked.

'Sure.' The shopkeeper ripped open the bag and laid the hands out for him.

They were not like gloves, because they did not cover the hands all round, but merely lay on top and were fastened by a strap underneath and another round the wrist. Just the tips of the fingers fitted into sockets so that the rubber fingers would not dangle about uselessly. Peter tried them on.

'You can't expect a perfect fit,' the shopkeeper said, 'because of course they don't make them in different sizes. If they're too big, just tighten the strap underneath and pull the one that goes round your wrist up your arm a bit.'

He helped him to put them on. They were rather big, but with them pulled well up the hands and over his wrists they were not bad at all, Peter decided. He would have them, if he could afford them. They were just as good as the magnificent mask, they had what looked like real hair growing along the backs, really satisfying long claws with just enough red on the ends to look as if they had torn into somebody's flesh, and what was more the red was actually painted to look as if it were still wet.

'Try the effect of both the mask and the hands,' suggested the shopkeeper, pointing towards a mirror on the wall behind the door, so Peter did. That was much better, especially in the fairly dim light inside the shop. Absolutely terrifying, almost.

'Wrap them up for you?' asked the shopkeeper.

'No, I'll take them as they are,' said Peter.

'Pardon?' The mask was not adjusted quite correctly, so his voice had been rather muffled.

Peter straightened the mask round his face so that his mouth was in the right place. 'No thanks. How much?'

He paid the money and left the shop wearing his new possessions, because he just happened to have noticed Billy Fidler leaning against the pillar box outside, looking the other way.

He ran out of the shop, crept round the side of the pillar box then slowly reached out a hand to touch Billy on the shoulder. Billy turned, as he expected him to do.

'That's pretty good,' said Billy, standing up. He looked Peter over critically. 'I like the hands.' Then he peered closer. 'Oh – it's Peter.'

'What do you think of it, then?' asked Peter.

'Pretty good. I could only really tell who you were by the clothes. It needs to be darker, though. I mean, you don't expect to come across a werewolf in daylight, so it looks just like a horrible mask and a pair of hands just now. If it was dark, though, and you suddenly came at me, that would really give me a nasty turn, I can tell you. Can I try them on?'

Peter didn't mind showing off his new acquisitions, and in any case he wanted to find out if what Billy had said was true. When Billy put them on, he found that it was. They were very good indeed, very effective for what they were, money well spent. But it was still unfortunately true that in broad daylight, on the pavement outside a row of shops with a pillar box just next to them, the mask was just a mask, and the hands were obviously artificial: not at all bad, though.

'Try them out on her,' advised Peter, seeing Wendy Glover approaching with her mother. She was a girl at their school who always seemed to frighten quite easily.

Billy obediently popped behind the pillar box, and as Wendy and her mother drew level suddenly jumped out in front of them. Wendy's mother drew her daughter a little closer to her with disdain.

'Billy Fidler, I should think,' remarked Wendy primly to her mother as they continued along the pavement. She turned after they had walked a few paces. 'A bit silly, I think,' she said loudly.

'I tell you, it'd be a different story if it was dark,' said Billy firmly, taking the mask and the hands off again and giving them back to Peter. 'You try it, and see if I'm not right.'

Peter slipped the items into his pockets and went

home, taking them upstairs and placing them carefully in the drawer of his dressing table, trying not to fold them and cause creases to develop in them.

It began to grow dark quite early that evening, so at the first opportunity Peter slipped off upstairs, stood in front of the mirror and tried the mask on again without switching on his bedroom light. In the dusk, it looked beautifully eerie. When he strapped the werewolf hands on to his own and then tried the effect in full, he almost managed to frighten himself, it looked so real that figure ready to leap out at him from the mirror.

Then he knew what was lacking, and ran downstairs into the kitchen, hurrying back up to his bedroom with a little pocket torch in his hands. This time he drew the curtains as well, and when the room was pitch black held the torch just underneath his chin and switched it on suddenly.

This time he really did jump in fright. In front of him was a monster, really horrible, writhing and drooling with just a hint of blood on the tips of its fangs and from its claws more blood shining in the light as if freshly drawn from a victim. He moved his left hand across his mouth as though trying to wipe it clean, and it was so realistic that he was glad to know that downstairs both of his parents were in the house.

'Well, well,' he said aloud, very pleased now, and hurried to switch on the electric light.

He put out the torch, sat on his bed and watched himself in the mirror as he removed first the hands and then the mask. It was almost a relief to be able to see him return to his normal self again. The only thing was, when would he ever have the opportunity to try these things out properly?

His father was calling from downstairs. 'Peter!'

'What?'

'Would you like to do something for me?'

'What?'

'Come down, and I'll tell you.'

Peter was about to replace his toys in the drawer again, thought better of it and stuffed them into his pockets instead, with the torch. If his father wanted him to go out, this might be just the opportunity he had been wondering about. He went downstairs, to find his father waiting for him in the hall.

'I've just remembered a couple of errands I'd like doing. You know the envelopes I've been putting through people's doors, collecting for the children's homes?'

'Yes.' Good, his father did want him to go out, then.

'There are two houses I called to collect them from last night, but the occupants were out. Just those two. Would you mind popping round to see if they're in tonight and collect them for me if they are? Take this with you —' and he handed over a little card of identity which stated that Peter's father was an author-ized collector for the children's homes — 'and explain who you are. They'll know you anyway, I expect, but take it just in case.'

'Which houses are they?'

'Number eighteen, along our road, Mr and Mrs Hubbard, then number forty-seven Devonshire Road. He's new, so I don't know his name.'

'No trouble,' said Peter. 'Won't take me ten minutes, if that.'

'OK then. Remember, it's the children's homes envelopes you're asking for,' his father called after him.

'I know,' said Peter, hurrying.

Once he was clear of the house he carefully drew out of his pockets the mask, and put it on, then the hands, then with the little torch held ready he set off down the street.

Number eighteen was not far away, but as he walked towards it Peter realized that there was nobody out on the street but himself. It was nicely dark by now, and the sky was clouded over, but all at once a cloud slid to one side and he saw that somewhere up there was not only the moon but a full one at that. Just the right sort of night for a werewolf to be abroad, he was thinking as the cloud glided back into place again, so he adjusted the mask so that the eyes and the mouth were in the right places, and pulled up the hairy hands as far as they would go. Then he continued briskly towards number eighteen, where he knocked on the door, pocket torch at the ready.

For a while there was no answer, then he heard the chain behind the door rattle, then a pause.

'Who is it?' he heard a woman's voice ask from inside.

'I've come for the envelope for the children's homes,' he said loudly.

'Just a minute.'

There was another pause, and he assumed that Mrs Hubbard was trying to find the envelope so that she could put tenpence inside it before opening the door. He got ready. Then the chain rattled a second time, and the door opened. As the figure of Mrs Hubbard appeared, he switched on the torch, directly under his chin.

Mrs Hubbard started and stepped back. Peter stood motionless with the light unwavering underneath his chin. There was a gasp, Mrs Hubbard clutched at her chest, then the door slammed shut and he heard the chain rattle again and then a bolt clunk into place.

That was very good, Peter was thinking. He did think of knocking on the door again, this time with his mask off, but thought better of it. She might not come to the door twice. So now for whoever it was who lived at number forty-seven Devonshire Road.

This was a large, gloomy house, with some kind of tall fir trees growing in the front garden behind a thick hedge. He did not remember ever having visited this house before. He opened the wooden gate and walked up the path, to find the front door was not at the front of the house but at the side, with more thick hedge growing in front of it on the opposite side of the narrow path. He wondered how anyone ever managed to carry furniture into the house when the path was as narrow as that.

He did not need to flash his torch to find the bell-push, because it was one of those illuminated ones, with a name on a card underneath it. *Luke Anthrope*, it said. So that was the name of the man who lived there, he thought; what an unusual name. He pressed the bell, and at once could hear an angry buzzing from somewhere inside, not like a bell at all. Feeling secure and safe behind his mask, when there was no answer he pressed the button again, and this time he heard a man's voice from inside the hall of this dark house. That rather surprised him, since there were no lights switched on that he could see.

'Go round the back,' it said hoarsely.

He walked further along the path to find a tall wooden gate, which opened easily, so he passed through it to see the back door of the house, and knocked on it. The door opened just as the moon came out again, but he was ready for it and had the torch under his chin immediately. Mr Anthrope did not frighten easily, however. He was a short man, with a thick beard and moustache, and he just stood there regarding Peter steadily.

'I've come for the envelope for the children's homes,' explained Peter, switching his torch off since it was obviously having no effect.

'Ah yes,' said Mr Anthrope, but made no move to go and fetch it.

'I've got a card here,' said Peter, fumbling in his pocket with some difficulty since the hand masks rather got in the way. 'It's my father's really, but it proves that you can give the envelope to me.'

The short man continued to regard him without moving. 'Switch that torch on again,' he said, so Peter did.

'Do you know why you never see two robins on a Christmas card?' the man asked him suddenly.

Peter did not.

'It's because if you ever find two robins together, they fight each other to the death. Did you know that? You can only ever find one robin in one place at a time. The same with one or two other creatures.'

Peter had no idea of what this Mr Anthrope was getting at. He had made no mention of robins. Robins had nothing to do with it. And what other creatures?

The man's face was beginning to change rather strangely in the moonlight, which was now shining full upon him. If was as if his beard was growing more straggly, somehow, and the face becoming more lined, and his lips seemed somehow to be thinner and more drawn back over his teeth. Peter only just noticed, too, now that the light was brighter, how hairy this man's hands were. Peter turned off the torch, because he did not need it now.

Then Mr Anthrope did a very strange thing. He came right out to the edge of his doorstep and leaned forward towards Peter as if he was going to whisper something to him.

Then Mr Anthrope's mouth was somewhere near his ear, and Peter, always curious, strained to be able to hear what Mr Anthrope was about to whisper to him. He was astonished then to feel the bones in the side of his neck crunching, and blood running down inside his shirt. He didn't even have time to cry out before long nails were tearing at his flesh.

Eels

JOHN GORDON

Rosemary was ten when she was smothered by Aunt Jenny and fed to the eels.

Oh, dear me, how easy it was. Poor lamb, to go so sweetly. But I was very angry at the time. 'And the strange thing is,' said Miss Jenny Jervis aloud, 'I am a single lady without brothers or sisters, so I'm not really her aunt.'

'Everyone knows that,' said Mrs Berry. 'When's that blasted bus coming?' They were waiting at Church Bridge for the bingo bus to take them to Terrington out across the fens.

'But she always called me auntie – I can't think why.'

'And I can't think why you suddenly started to come to bingo. Gambling – that ain't like you, Jenny Jervis.'

Miss Jervis simpered. 'Maybe I'm feeling lucky, Phoebe.'

Heavens, yes. Very lucky. First Rosemary with the

eels, and now Rosemary's mother has passed away. By accident. So she'll never come looking for her darling little Rosemary again. How very convenient. No need of eels for her.

'I feel fresh as a daisy today,' said Miss Jervis. 'Free as a bird.'

'Damned if you don't look it.' Mrs Berry cast an eye over the flowered dress, the gloves and the white hat with a hint of veil across Miss Jervis's brow. 'It's not a wedding, you know – only bloody bingo.'

'It pleases you to be blunt, Phoebe,' said Miss Jervis, 'but other people are not so unkind. Rosemary for one – although,' she added modestly, 'I still can't think why she has always been so nice to me.'

'Don't come that with me,' said Mrs Berry. 'You know well enough.' The bus came drifting along the waterside. 'And for God's sake help me up these blasted steps.'

Mrs Berry, unlike Miss Jervis, was fat and her hips were so bad she could hardly lift her feet. She handed over her stick before she grasped the handrail. 'And wipe that stupid expression off of your face, Jenny Jervis. The girl calls you auntie because she loves you, God knows why.'

Miss Jervis held the stick by the middle and kept it clear of the ground in case germs ran up it and into her gloves. 'I've only been doing my duty by the girl,' she said.

'Duty be blowed.' Mrs Berry's grunt was muffled in her fat bosom as she heaved her way upwards. 'Who cares about duty? – you don't, for one.'

'You are wrong there, Phoebe.' Miss Jervis regarded the broad rear end.

Quite wrong. My duty was to dispatch the child. She should never have been born, so it was her destiny, the darling.

'I have a strong sense of duty,' she said.

'Squit! You have a strong sense of looking after number one – like the rest of us.'

'Here's your stick, dear.' Miss Jervis handed it over, and dusted off the tips of her gloves.

'And don't call me dear!' Mrs Berry had found a seat and was peeling the wrapper from a pack of king size. 'I'm not in a bloody rest home yet.'

The bus began to move, and Miss Jervis looked down into the river as it slid by.

Silly to call it a river, but they all do. It's a drainage cut, as they very well know, because the water's quite still and not like a river at all. Fortunate, really, because I knew just where Rosemary was until the eels had finished with her. It was quite hygienic. All I had to do was wrap up the bones and put them in the dustbin a few at a time until there was nothing left. Nothing.

'What are you smiling at?'

'Just thoughts,' said Miss Jervis.

'Once a schoolteacher, always a bloody school-teacher. You're just the same as you was when you was a kid, Jenny Jervis. Anyone could've seen you was never really going to put that school behind you.'

'Don't get so cross with me, Phoebe. There's nothing wrong with being a teacher.'

Headmistress, actually, when I retired. And what did you every do, fat Phoebe?

'I love being with children,' she said.

'You never showed much sign of it.' Mrs Berry plugged a cigarette into her plump face and waved a flame at it. 'You never got married, did you? Never had no children of your own, never hardly got away from this village where you was born.'

'I was away at training college for three years, don't forget.'

'Training college.' Mrs Berry clicked her tongue. 'That must've been a riot.'

Phoebe, Phoebe, I had a baby.

The rhyme sprang to Miss Jervis's mind and made her smile.

I had a baby, and I don't mean maybe.

She looked out of the window.

Mrs Berry, who had been watching her from the corner of her eye, said, 'You can't tell me you girls didn't get up to some fun and games when you was away from home.'

Miss Jervis raised her eyebrows. 'We were training to be *teachers*, Phoebe, so nothing very terrible happened.'

Except, of course, I had a baby girl and couldn't come home for a while.

'And anyway,' she smiled, 'even if there had been something I was ashamed of I wouldn't have let anyone know, would I?'

'You're grinning like a cat that's had the cream,' said Mrs Berry.

'Am I? I wonder why.'

And you may well turn away with that disgusted expression on your face, fat Phoebe, because now there's no chance at all you'll ever find out anything.

Using both hands, Miss Jervis smoothed her dress firmly across her thighs and spoke to herself very clearly.

And wouldn't you just love to know that the daughter I had was adopted and grew up to have a daughter of her own? And that little girl was Rosemary – so I'm not her auntie; I'm her granny. I'm a granny, Phoebe, just like you.

'Anyway,' she said mischievously, 'I don't suppose my sins will ever come home to roost now.'

'Not that you ever had none.'

'Not that I ever had any,' said Miss Jervis primly, but she could not help a shiver, because her sin very nearly had come home to roost. Not long since.

But you don't know that, Phoebe. I had my baby adopted the day after she was born and I thought she was gone for ever.

Miss Jervis closed her eyes.

And then . . . after all those years . . . she found me!

'It was a terrible moment' – the words came out before she could stop them.

'What was?'

'I mean it must be a terrible moment when your sins catch up with you.' She gave a little grimace.

You'll never catch me out, Phoebe fatbum. Not now. Rosemary has gone, and now my dear daughter is also no longer with us.

'Did you read about that awful plane crash?' she asked.

'What about it?' Mrs Berry was annoyed at the sudden change of subject.

'Well, I was just wondering about those poor people. Their sins caught up with them, didn't they?'

My daughter, for one. She dumped that Rosemary on me, and threatened to give away my secret if I didn't take her, just so she could gad about with her boyfriend. Well, now she's gone, her and her boyfriend. Serve 'em both right.

Miss Jervis had read the passenger list. 'It's so sad,' she said.

'Not that you look it.'

'Well, it's such a lovely day.'

And I'm so lucky. Nobody left to ask questions about Rosemary; no more blackmail from Rosemary's mother.

'I can't never fathom you out.' Mrs Berry, because her fat legs pressed into the seat in front, let ash dribble into her lap. 'You was headmistress, with your own little house by the river, everything you ever wanted – and then you had to go and saddle yourself with that kid Rosemary. At your time of life.'

'It was because of a friend from the old days.'

A friend! I mean my dear daughter – happily no longer with us.

'And my little home was just perfect for the two of us.'

'Well, kids are kids – I wonder you could stand having your place messed up.'

'But it was no problem, Phoebe, no problem at all.'

Until the stupid child began to whine for the mother who didn't want her.

'Because she is such a sweet little girl,' said Miss Jervis.

Was a little girl. And sweet at the end. She drifted away so softly under her pillow she could hardly have felt its touch.

'So sweet,' sighed Miss Jervis.

'Sweet as a sugar plum, no doubt, but it was never your way to burden yourself.'

'You have a cruel tongue, Phoebe, but my deeds speak louder than words.'

'Hark at little Miss Prim. Never done a thing wrong in her whole life – I *don't* think.'

It was said so knowingly that Miss Jervis felt a touch of anxiety. 'I don't understand you,' she said.

'I know something you done, Jenny Jervis . . . something you was ashamed of.'

Mrs Berry's eyes suddenly had such a hard glint that Miss Jervis looked away.

But it couldn't be Rosemary. Everybody believed me when I said she'd gone home to her mother.

'You was a naughty girl once.' Mrs Berry was sly, and waited to see the effect. 'That's made you go pale, ain't it?'

'There's nothing on my conscience, Phoebe.'

'Well, there should be.'

Miss Jervis sat quite still.

'You gone white just like you did then. First you

went white, then you went red and then you started to cry and said it wasn't your fault. You'd have done anything to stop other people knowing what you done. And I was the one who could've shamed you, Jenny Jervis.'

Miss Jervis made a tiny movement with her gloves.

'I see you remember it now – that day when we was kids and you snitched some sweets from a girl's desk.' Her eyes were on Miss Jervis. 'And I seen you do it.'

'Is that all?' Miss Jervis let out her breath.

'*All*, you say. *All*.'

'I was only trying to put her books straight.' Miss Jervis was annoyed to find that her mouth had gone dry.

'Then why did you snivel and grovel and promise me anything so long as I wouldn't tell? Books my foot!'

'But . . .'

'No buts. You're still making excuses. You never did give a thought to that poor girl you was thieving from – all you cared about was that you shouldn't be shamed. That's what you was afraid of – shame.'

Miss Jervis took a handkerchief from her glove. 'I think you're trying to spoil my little outing, Phoebe.'

'And now it's tears. Just as it always was. You haven't changed one little bit.'

Miss Jervis blew her nose. 'I'm relieved that I haven't any worse skeletons in my cupboard,' she said. 'Perhaps I'm lucky.'

And she was. She won at bingo. She could do nothing wrong, and knew it in her bones. So when the old woman sitting next to her was careless with her purse, Miss Jervis dipped her fingers into it and came out with a note.

She was putting it into her handbag before she realized she had been spotted. A finger was pointed, and silence spread outwards from where she sat until the hall was full of waxworks with every head turned her way.

'But I was only helping her to buy her tickets,' she said, and the silence deepened.

Outside, Mrs Berry said, 'Get on the bus and shut up.' She made Miss Jervis sit next to the window and sat beside her to wedge her in and prevent her getting to the aisle. 'I don't want you flinging yourself off of this bus and making more trouble for everybody.'

Miss Jervis's voice had almost gone. 'I was only going to give her some change for her tickets,' she whispered. Her throat hurt.

'Just stay quiet.' Mrs Berry was smoking hard. 'Nobody wants to hear you.'

There had been a lot of chatter and laughter on the bus going out. Now the sound of voices barely rose above the rumble of the wheels, and all the women watched in silence when it drew up at the waterside and Mrs Berry and Miss Jervis got off.

'You look a bit tottery.' Mrs Berry, leaning on her stick, took pity on her. 'Would you like to have a cup of tea with me?'

'No thank you, Phoebe.'

It was dusk, but the air was still warm. Mrs Berry tried to make conversation. 'Lovely evening,' she said. 'Lots of midges, though.' They could just be seen above the pale surface of the water, dancing in congregations. Before long they would be invisible. Miss Jervis watched them but said nothing.

'Don't worry about it,' said Mrs Berry. 'It won't seem so bad in the morning.' She breathed heavily, as though kindliness cost her an effort. 'None of us is perfect.'

Miss Jervis murmured good night, and Mrs Berry watched until she had trailed slowly across the road to her front door, fumbled for her key and let herself in.

Mrs Berry walked painfully away. 'Stupid bloody woman,' she grunted. 'Looks as if she wants to do away with herself. Well, she shouldn't have done what she done in the first place.'

Miss Jervis did, in fact, have death in mind. How could she face anyone ever again? She put on her nightdress but did not go to bed. Instead she sat by the empty fireplace until the daylight had washed itself out of the sky, and then she opened her front door and went barefoot across the road to the waterside. She had unpinned her hair, and the grey strands hung loosely. It no longer mattered.

She went carefully, out of habit, down the grassy bank, and before her toes touched the water she leant over and looked down. The movement allowed her unpinned hair to brush her face, and saved her life.

The touch of her hair swinging against her face made her automatically lift her head to brush it away, and it was then she saw the midges. Phoebe Berry was right; there were clouds of them. As they gyrated they made shapes as wispy as bubbles on the point of bursting. If creatures so flimsy continued to exist, why should she die?

Miss Jervis turned away, and slipped. She should have known how treacherous the bank was because it was here she had weighted Rosemary for the eels. But now she had let both feet slide into the water, and she had to struggle before she managed to get a tight enough grip on the grass to crawl up the bank.

The edge of her nightgown was wet and clung to her ankles as she crossed the road, and as soon as she was indoors she changed it.

'Now a nice hot cup of tea, Miss Jervis,' she said, lecturing herself, 'and no more nonsense.'

The sound of her own voice made her feel stronger. She would go to bingo again and brazen it out. She would be generous, so generous that they would all be overwhelmed with guilt for accusing her. And then *she* would forgive *them*, and they would respect her even more.

'Because you stand for something in this village,' she told herself, 'and always will.' She dried her feet vigorously. 'Now off to bed with you.'

Despite the rubbing, her feet and ankles remained cold so she took a hot water bottle with her. The bed was soon luxuriously warm, and her mind was at rest.

She slept so soundly that she awoke with cramp down one side and nothing would ease the pain until she moved about her room. It was still dark, and she pulled aside the curtains, as she had so often done, to look at the water and be certain that nothing was disturbing Rosemary. That worry was done with for ever.

It was a summer's night and enough light filtered from the sky to show the smooth face of the river, and even the track of bent grass she had left in the verge. And her wet footprints still led to the door.

'The sun will be my friend,' she said. 'All will be dry soon.'

She slid back into bed. The water bottle was cold and she pushed it to one side, but its coolness lingered. She thrust it further away and gasped with annoyance. It must have burst because a cold wetness was on her feet. She sat up and reached down. The chill rubber was clammy. Slimy. It slipped under her fingers as though it was moving. She flung it out of bed. It slapped the floor, but she had used too much violence because she heard it slither further.

'Damn!' Miss Jervis never swore, but she was angry. The water bottle would be leaking all over the floor, and she also had to change the bed. 'Damn!'

She threw aside the bedcover, but the damp sheet had twisted around her feet. She was reaching down to untangle herself when her heart thudded. She was not alone in the room. Silhouetted against the window was a shape.

Fear had made Miss Jervis cringe backwards, but suddenly she leant forward, and now her heart was pounding with anger. The silhouette was human. But it was neither tall nor broad. It was a child. One of her pupils. Some stupid prank.

'Get out!' It was a classroom order. 'Get out at once!'

The child, however, came forward, slowly and heavily. Its footsteps dragged as if with a great weight.

'I'll see you pay for this!'

Miss Jervis gathered herself to lunge, but her feet would not obey her. They would not move. She reached down. The bed was wet and cold, but it was not the sheet that had trapped her feet. Something slippery had coiled itself around her ankles. And it was moving. She felt something slide between her toes and tenderly begin to stroke her leg.

'No!' she cried. 'No!'

Feverishly, trying to pull back at the same time, she reached down. Her fingers plunged into a nest of eels.

Miss Jervis screamed. She flung her hands to the bedrail to haul herself free. She struggled. The cold grip tightened and held her legs still. She could not move.

She was whimpering as the child came closer. Its footsteps slithered and squelched and it brought the darkness of deep water into the room. It stopped by the bedside, and a hand reached out to hold hers. If it was a hand. Miss Jervis never knew.

The child's fingers writhed and were slimy. And the child's head, when it bent over her, had many damp tendrils of hair that, eager and slippery, reached out to busily caress her face, loving her.

When the sun came up and filled the room with warmth, Miss Jervis lay quite still. Her nightgown, however, heaved with a life of its own.

Jonathan Harker's Journal

from *Dracula*
BRAM STOKER

I suppose I must have fallen asleep; I hope so, but I
fear, for all that followed was startlingly real – so
real that now, sitting here in the broad, full sunlight
of the morning, I cannot in the least believe that it
was all sleep.

I was not alone. The room was the same, unchanged
in any way since I came into it; I could see along the
floor, in the brilliant moonlight, my own footsteps
marked where I had disturbed the long accumulation
of dust. In the moonlight opposite me were three
young women, ladies by their dress and manner. I
thought at the time that I must be dreaming when I
saw them, for, though the moonlight was behind
them, they threw no shadow on the floor. They came
close to me and looked at me for some time and then
whispered together. Two were dark, and had high
aquiline noses, like the Count's, and great dark, piercing eyes, that seemed to be almost red when contrasted

with the pale yellow moon. The other was fair, as fair as can be, with great, wavy masses of golden hair and eyes like pale sapphires. I seemed somehow to know her face, and to know it in connection with some dreamy fear, but I could not recollect at the moment how or where. All three had brilliant white teeth, that shone like pearls against the ruby of their voluptuous lips. There was something about them that made me uneasy, some longing and at the same time some deadly fear. I felt in my heart a wicked, burning desire that they would kiss me with those red lips. It is not good to note this down, lest some day it should meet Mina's eyes and cause her pain; but it is the truth. They whispered together, and then they all three laughed – such a silvery, musical laugh, but as hard as though the sound never could have come through the softness of human lips. It was like the intolerable, tingling sweetness of water-glasses when played on by a cunning hand. The fair girl shook her head coquettishly, and the other two urged her on. One said:

'Go on! You are first, and we shall follow; yours is the right to begin.' The other added:

'He is young and strong; there are kisses for us all.' I lay quiet, looking out under my eyelashes in an agony of delightful anticipation. The fair girl advanced and bent over me till I could feel the movement of her breath upon me. Sweet it was in one sense, honey-sweet, and sent the same tingling through the nerves as her voice, but with a bitter underlying the sweet, a bitter offensiveness, as one smells in blood.

I was afraid to raise my eyelids, but looked out and saw perfectly under the lashes. The fair girl went on her knees and bent over me, fairly gloating. There was a deliberate voluptuousness which was both thrilling and repulsive, and as she arched her neck she actually licked her lips like an animal, till I could see in the moonlight the moisture shining on the scarlet lips and on the red tongue as it lapped the white sharp teeth. Lower and lower went her head as the lips went below the range of my mouth and chin and seemed about to fasten on my throat. Then she paused, and I could hear the churning sound of her tongue as it licked her teeth and lips, and could feel the hot breath on my neck. Then the skin of my throat began to tingle as one's flesh does when the hand that is to tickle it approaches nearer — nearer. I could feel the soft, shivering touch of the lips on the supersensitive skin of my throat, and the hard dents of two sharp teeth, just touching and pausing there. I closed my eyes in a languorous ecstasy and waited — waited with beating heart.

But at that instant another sensation swept through me as quick as lightning. I was conscious of the presence of the Count, and of his being as if lapped in a storm of fury. As my eyes opened involuntarily I saw his strong hand grasp the slender neck of the fair woman and with giant's power draw it back, the blue eyes transformed with fury, the white teeth champing with rage, and the fair cheeks blazing red with passion. But the Count! Never did I imagine such wrath and fury, even in the demons of the pit. His eyes were positively blazing. The red light in them was lurid, as if the flames of hell-fire blazed behind them. His face was deathly pale, and the lines of it were hard like drawn wires; the thick eyebrows that met over the nose now seemed like a heaving bar of white-hot metal. With a fierce sweep of his arm, he hurled the woman from. him, and then motioned to the others, as though he were beating them back; it was the same imperious gesture that I had seen used to the wolves. In a voice which, though low and almost a whisper, seemed to cut through the air and then ring round the room, he exclaimed:

'How dare you touch him, any of you? How dare you cast eyes on him when I had forbidden it? Back, I tell you all! This man belongs to me! Beware how you meddle with him, or you'll have to deal with me.' The fair girl, with a laugh of ribald coquetry, turned to answer him:

'You yourself never loved; you never love!' On this the other women joined, and such a mirthless, hard, soulless laughter rang through the room that it almost made me faint to hear; it seemed like the pleasure of fiends. Then the Count turned, after looking at my face attentively, and said in a soft whisper:

'Yes, I too can love; you yourselves can tell it from the past. Is it not so? Well, now I promise you that when I am done with him, you shall kiss him at your will. Now go! go! I must awaken him, for there is work to be done.'

'Are we to have nothing tonight?' said one of them, with a low laugh, as she pointed to the bag which he had thrown upon the floor, and which moved as though there were some living thing within it. For answer he nodded his head. One of the women jumped forward and opened it. If my ears did not deceive me there was a gasp and a low wail, as of a half-smothered child. The women closed round, whilst I was aghast with horror; but as I looked they disappeared, and with them the dreadful bag. There was no door near them, and they could not have passed me without my noticing. They simply seemed to fade into the rays of the moonlight and pass out through the window, for I could see outside the dim, shadowy forms for a moment before they entirely faded away.

Then the horror overcame me, and I sank down unconscious.

Bath Night

ANTHONY HOROWITZ

She didn't like the bath from the start.

Isabel was at home the Saturday they delivered it and wondered how the fat, metal beast was ever going to make it up one flight of stairs, around the corner and into the bathroom. The two scrawny workmen didn't seem to have much idea either. Thirty minutes, four gashed knuckles and a hundred swear words later it seemed to be hopelessly wedged and it was only when Isabel's father lent a hand that they were able to free it. But then one of the stubby legs caught the wallpaper and tore it and that led to another argument right in front of the workmen, her mother and father blaming each other like they always did.

'I told you to measure it.'

'I did measure it.'

'Yes. But you said the legs came off.'

'No. That's what you said.'

It was so typical of her parents to buy that bath, Isabel thought. Anyone else would have been into the West End to one of the smart department stores. Pick something out of the showroom. Out with the credit card. Delivery and free installation in six weeks and thank you very much.

But Jeremy and Susan Harding weren't like that. Ever since they had bought their small, turn-of-the-century house in Muswell Hill, North London, they had devoted their holidays to getting it just right. And since they were both teachers – he at a public school, she in a local primary – their holidays were frequent and long.

And so the dining-room table had come from an antique shop in Hungerford, the chairs that surrounded it from a house sale in Hove. The kitchen cupboards had been rescued from a skip in Macclesfield. And their double bed had been a rusting, tangled heap when they had found it in the barn of a French farmhouse outside Boulogne. So many weekends. So many hours spent searching, measuring, imagining, haggling and arguing.

That was the worst of it. As far as Isabel could see, her parents didn't seem to get any pleasure out of all these antiques. They fought constantly – in the shops, in the market places, even at the auctions. Once her father had got so heated he had actually broken the Victorian chamber pot they had been arguing about and of course he'd had to buy it anyway. It was in the hall now, glued back together again, the all-too-visible cracks an unpleasant image of their twelve-year-old marriage.

The bath was Victorian too. Isabel had been with her parents when they bought it – at an architectural salvage yard in West London. 'Made in about 1890,' the dealer had told them. 'A real beauty. It's still got its own taps . . .'

It certainly didn't look beautiful as it squatted there on the stripped pine floor, surrounded by stops and washers and twisting lengths of pipe. It reminded Isabel of a pregnant cow, its great white belly hanging only inches off the ground. Its metal feet curved outwards, splayed, as if unable to bear the weight. And of course it had been decapitated. There was a single round hole where the taps would be and beneath it an ugly yellow stain in the white enamel where the water had trickled down for perhaps a hundred years, on its way to the plug-hole below. Isabel glanced at the tap, lying on its side next to the sink, a tangle of mottled brass that looked too big for the bath it was meant to sit on. There were two handles, marked with a black H and a C on faded ivory discs – but only one outlet. Isabel imagined the water thundering in. It would need to. The bath was very deep.

But nobody used the bath that night. Jeremy had said he would be able to connect it up himself but in the end he had found it was beyond him. Nothing fitted. It would have to be soldered. Unfortunately he wouldn't be able to get a plumber until Monday and of course it would add another forty pounds to the bill and when he told Susan that led to another argument. They ate their dinner in front of the television that night, letting the shallow laughter of a sitcom cover the chill silence in the room.

And then it was nine o'clock. 'You'd better go to bed early, darling. School tomorrow,' Susan said.

'Yes, Mum.' Isabel was twelve but her mother – a short and rather severe woman – treated her sometimes as if she were much younger. Maybe it came from teaching in a primary school.

Isabel undressed and washed quickly – hands, face, neck, teeth, in that order. The face that gazed out at her from the gilded mirror above the sink wasn't an unattractive one, she thought, except for the annoying pimple on her nose . . . a punishment for the Mars Bar ice-cream she'd eaten the day before. Long brown hair and blue eyes (her mother's), a thin face with narrow cheek-bones and chin (her father's). She had been fat until she was nine but now she was getting herself in shape. She'd never be a super-model. She was too fond of ice-cream for that. But no fatty either, not like Belinda Price, her best friend at school who was doomed to a life of hopeless diets and baggy clothes.

The shape of the bath, over her shoulder, caught her eye and she realized suddenly that from the moment she had come into the bathroom she had been trying to avoid looking at it. Why? She put her toothbrush down, turned round and examined it. She didn't like it. Her first impression had been right. It was so big and ugly with its dull enamel and dribbling stain over the plug-hole. And it seemed – it was a stupid thought but now it was there she couldn't make it go away – it seemed to be *waiting* for her. She half-smiled at her own foolishness. And then she noticed something else.

There was a small puddle of water in the bottom of the bath. As she moved her head, it caught the light and she saw it clearly. Isabel's first thought was to look up at the ceiling. There had to be a leak, some-where upstairs, in the attic. How else could water have got into a bath whose taps were lying on their side next to the sink? But there was no leak. Isabel leant forward and ran her third finger along the bottom of the bath. The water was warm.

'I must have splashed it in there myself,' she thought. 'As I was washing my face . . .'

She flicked the light off and left the room, crossing the landing to her bedroom on the other side of her parents'. Somewhere in her mind she knew that it wasn't true, that she could never have splashed water from the sink into the bath. But it wasn't an important question. In fact it was ridiculous. She curled up in bed and closed her eyes.

But an hour later her thumb was still rubbing circles against her third finger and it was a long time before she slept.

'Bath night!' her father said when she got home from school the next day. He was in a good mood, smiling broadly as he shuffled together the ingredients for that night's dinner.

'Where's Mum?' Isabel asked.

'Shopping.' She had offended him. Isabel saw that in his one-word answer and the way he turned away from her, sliding some sliced onions into a pan of hot oil. He wanted her to share his enthusiasm, to talk about the bath. The onions sizzled angrily.

'So you got it plumbed in then.'

'Yes.' He turned back again. 'It cost fifty pounds – don't tell your mother. The plumber was here for two hours.' He smiled and blinked several times and Isabel was reminded of something she had once been told by the brother of a friend who went to Highgate. Her father was a very thin man with prematurely grey hair and a face that always seemed to be turned down. At school, his nickname was Grumpy. Why did boys have to be so cruel?

She reached out and squeezed his arm. 'That's great, Dad,' she said. 'I'll have a bath after dinner. What are you making?'

'Lasagne. Your mum's gone out to get some wine.'

It was a more pleasant evening. Isabel had got a part in her school play – Lady Montague in *Romeo and Juliet*. Susan had found a ten-pound note in the pocket of a jacket she hadn't worn for years. Jeremy had been asked to take a party of boys to Paris at the end of term. Good news oiled the machinery of the family and for once everything turned smoothly. After dinner, Isabel did half an hour's homework, kissed her parents goodnight and went upstairs. To the bathroom.

The bath was ready now. Installed. Permanent. The taps with the black H and C protruded over the rim with the curve of a vulture's neck. A silver plug on a heavy chain slanted into the plug-hole. Her father had polished the brasswork, giving it a new gleam. He had put the towels back on the rail and a green bath-mat on the floor. Everything back to normal. And yet the room, the towels, the bath-mat seemed to have shrunk. The bath was too big. And it was waiting for her. She still couldn't get the thought out of her mind.

'Isabel. Stop being silly . . .!'

What's the first sign of madness? Talking to your-self. And the second sign? Answering back. Isabel let out a great sigh of breath and went over to the bath. She leant in and pushed the plug into the hole. Down-stairs, she could hear the television: *World in Action*, one of her father's favourite programmes. She reached out and turned on the hot tap, the metal squeaking slightly under her hand. Without pausing, she gave the cold tap a quarter turn. Now let's see if that plumber was worth his fifty quid.

For a moment, nothing happened. Then, deep down underneath the floor, something rumbled. There was a rattling in the pipe that grew louder and louder as it rose up but there was still no water. Then the tap coughed, the cough of an old man, of a heavy smoker. A bubble appeared, to be broken a moment later by a spurt of liquid. Isabel looked down in dismay.

Whatever had been spat into the bath was not water. It was an ugly red, the colour of rust. The taps spluttered again and coughed out more of the thick, treacly stuff. It bounced off the bottom of the bath and splattered against the sides. Isabel was beginning to feel sick and before the taps could deliver a third load of – whatever it was – into the bath, she seized hold of them and locked them both shut. She could feel the pipes rattling beneath her hands but then it was done. The shuddering stopped. The rest of the liquid was swallowed back into the network of pipes.

But still it wasn't over. The bottom of the bath was coated with the liquid that now slid unwillingly towards the plug-hole which swallowed it greedily. Isabel looked more closely. Was she going mad or was there something *inside* the plug-hole? Isabel was sure she had put the plug in but now it was half-in and half-out of the hole and she could see below.

There was something. It was like a white ball, turning slowly, collapsing in on itself, glistening wet and alive. And it was rising, making for the surface . . .

Isabel cried out. At the same time she leant over and jammed the plug back into the hole. Her hand touched the red liquid and she recoiled, feeling it, warm and clinging, against her skin.

And that was enough. She reeled back, yanked a towel off the rail and rubbed it against her hand so hard that it hurt. Then she threw open the bathroom door and ran downstairs.

Her parents were still watching television.

'What's the matter with you?' Jeremy asked. Isabel had explained what had happened, the words tumbling over each other in their hurry to get out, but it was as if her father hadn't listened. 'There's always a bit of rust with a new bath,' he went on. 'It's in the pipes. Run the water for a few minutes and it'll go.'

'It wasn't rust,' Isabel said.

'Maybe the boiler's playing up again,' Susan muttered.

'It's not the boiler.' Jeremy frowned. He had bought it second-hand and it had always been a sore point — particularly when it broke down.

'It was horrible,' Isabel insisted. 'It was like . . .' What had it been like? Of course, she had known all along. 'Well, it was like blood. It was just like blood. And there was something else. Inside the plug.'

'Oh for heaven's sake!' Jeremy was irritated now, missing his programme.

'Come on! I'll come up with you . . .' Susan pushed a pile of Sunday newspapers off the sofa — she was still reading them even though this was Monday evening — and got to her feet.

'Where's the TV control?' Jeremy found it in the corner of his armchair and turned the volume up.

Isabel and her mother went upstairs, back into the bathroom. Isabel looked at the towel lying crumpled where she had left it. A white towel. She had wiped her hands on it. She was surprised to see there was no trace of a stain.

'What a lot of fuss over a teaspoon of rust!' Susan was leaning over the bath. Isabel stepped forward and peered in nervously. But it was true. There was a shallow puddle of water in the middle and a few grains of reddish rust. 'You know there's always a little rust in the system,' her mother went on. 'It's that stupid boiler of your father's.' She pulled out the plug. 'Nothing in there either!' Finally, she turned on the tap. Clean, ordinary water gushed out in a reassuring torrent. No rattling. No gurgles. Nothing. 'There you are. It's sorted itself out.'

Isabel hung back, leaning miserably against the sink. Her mother sighed. 'You were making it all up, weren't you?' she said – but her voice was affectionate, not angry.

'No, Mum.'

'It seems a long way to go to get out of having a bath.'

'I wasn't . . .!'

'Never mind now. Clean your teeth and go to bed.' Susan kissed her. 'Good-night, dear. Sleep well.'

But that night Isabel didn't sleep at all.

She didn't have a bath the following night either. Jeremy Harding was out – there was a staff meeting at the school – and Susan was trying out a new recipe for a dinner party the following week-end. She spent the whole evening in the kitchen.

Nor did Isabel have a bath on Wednesday. That was three days in a row and she was beginning to feel more than uncomfortable. She liked to be clean. That was her nature and as much as she tried flannelling herself using the sink, it wasn't the same. And it didn't help that her father had used the bath on Tuesday morning and her mother on Tuesday and Wednesday and neither of them had noticed anything wrong. It just made her feel more guilty – and dirtier.

Then on Thursday morning someone made a joke at school – something about rotten eggs – and as her cheeks burned, Isabel decided enough was enough. What was she so afraid of anyway? A sprinkling of rust which her imagination had turned into . . . something else. Susan Harding was out that evening – she was learning Italian at night school – so Isabel and her father sat down together for their evening meal.

At nine o'clock they went their separate ways – he to the news, she upstairs.

'Goodnight, Dad.'

'Goodnight, Is.'

It had been a nice, companionable evening.

And there was the bath, waiting for her. Yes. It was waiting, as if to receive her. But this time Isabel didn't hesitate. If she was as brisk and business-like as possible, she had decided, then nothing would happen. She simply wouldn't give her imagination time to play tricks on her. So without even thinking about it, she slipped the plug into the hole, turned on the taps and added a squirt of avocado bubble bath for good measure. She undressed (her clothes were a useful mask, stopping her seeing the water as it filled) and only when she was quite naked did she turn round and look at the bath. It was fine. She could just see the water, a pale avocado green beneath a thick layer of foam. She stretched out her hand and felt the temperature. It was perfect: hot enough to steam up the mirror but not so hot as to scald. She turned off the taps. They dripped loudly as she remembered and went over to lock the door.

Yet still she hesitated. She was suddenly aware of her nakedness. It was as if she were in a room full of people. She shivered. 'You're being ridiculous,' she told herself. But still the question hung in the air with the steam from the water. It was like a nasty, unfunny riddle.

When are you at your most defenceless?

When you're naked, enclosed, lying on your back . . .

. . . in the bath.

'Ridiculous.' This time she actually said the word. And in one swift movement, a no-go-back decision, she got in.

The bath had tricked her – but she realized too late.

The water was not hot. It wasn't even warm. She had tested the temperature moments before. She had seen the steam rising. But the water was colder than anything Isabel had ever felt. It was like breaking through the ice on a pond on a midwinter's day. As she sank helplessly into the bath, felt the water slide over her legs and stomach, close in on her throat like a clamp, her breath was punched back and her heart seemed to stop in mid-beat. The cold hurt her. It cut into her. Isabel opened her mouth and screamed as loudly as she could. The sound was nothing more than a choked off whimper.

Isabel was being pulled under the water. Her neck hit the rim of the bath and slid down, her long hair floating away from her. The foam slid over her mouth, then over her nose. She tried to move but her arms and legs wouldn't obey the signals she sent them. Her bones had frozen. The room seemed to be getting dark.

But then, with one final effort, Isabel twisted round and threw herself up, over the edge. Water exploded everywhere, splashing down on to the floor. Then somehow she was lying down with foam all around her, sobbing and shivering, her skin completely white. She reached out and caught the corner of a towel, pulled it over her. Water trickled off her back and disappeared through the cracks in the floorboards.

Isabel lay like that for a long time. She had been scared . . . scared almost to death. But it wasn't just the change in the water that had done it. It wasn't just the bath itself – as ugly and menacing as it was. No. It was the sound she had heard as she heaved herself out and jack-knifed on to the floor. She had heard it inches away from her ear, in the bathroom, even though she was alone.

Somebody had laughed.

*

'You don't believe me, do you?'

Isabel was standing at the bus-stop with Belinda Price; fat, reliable Belinda, always there when you needed her, her best friend. A week had passed and all the time it had built up inside her, what had happened in the bathroom, the story of the bath. But still Isabel had kept it to herself. Why? Because she was afraid of being laughed at? Because she was afraid no one would believe her? Because, simply, she was afraid. In that week she had done no work . . . at school or at home. She had been told off twice in class. Her clothes and her hair were in a state. Her eyes were dark with lack of sleep. But in the end she couldn't hold it back any more. She had told Belinda.

And now the other girl shrugged. 'I've heard of haunted houses,' she muttered. 'And haunted castles. I've even heard of a haunted car. But a haunted bath . . .?'

'It happened, just like I said.'

'Maybe you think it happened. If you think something hard enough it can often . . .'

'It wasn't my imagination,' Isabel interrupted.

Then the bus came and the two girls got on, showing their passes to the driver. They took their seats on the top deck, near the back. They always sat in the same place without quite knowing why.

'You can't keep coming round to my place,' Belinda said. 'I'm sorry, Bella, but my mum's beginning to ask what's going on.'

'I know.' Isabel sighed. She had managed to go

round to Belinda's house three nights running and
had showered there, grateful for the hot, rushing
water. She had told her parents that she and Belinda
were working on a project. But Belinda was right. It
couldn't go on for ever.

The bus reached the traffic lights and turned on to
the main road. Belinda screwed up her face, deep in
thought. All the teachers said how clever she was, not
just because she worked hard but because she let you
see it. 'You say the bath is an old one,' she said at last.

'Yes?'

'Do you know where your parents got it?'

Isabel thought back. 'Yes. It came from a place in
Fulham. I've been there with them before.'

'Then why don't you go there and ask them about
it? I mean, if it is haunted there must be a reason.
There's always a reason, isn't there?'

'You mean . . . someone might have died in it or
something?' The thought made Isabel shiver.

'Yes. My gran had a heart attack in the bath. It
didn't kill her though . . .'

'You're right!' The bus was climbing up the hill
now. Muswell Hill Broadway was straight ahead.
Isabel gathered her things. 'I could go there on Saturday. Will you come too?'

'My mum and dad wouldn't let me.'

'You can tell them you're at my place. And I'll tell
my parents I'm at yours.'

'What if they check?'

'They never do.' The thought made Isabel sad. Her

parents never did wonder where she was, never seemed to worry about her. They were too wrapped up in themselves.

'Well . . . I don't know . . .'

'Please, Belinda. On Saturday. I'll give you a call.'

That night the bath played its worst trick yet.

Isabel hadn't wanted to have a bath. During dinner she'd made a point of telling her parents how tired she was, how she was looking forward to an early night. But her parents were tired too. They'd argued earlier in the evening . . . they were going to the cinema the following week-end and couldn't decide on the film. The atmosphere around the table had been distinctly jagged and Isabel found herself wondering just how much longer the family could stay together. Divorce. It was a horrible word, like an illness. Some of her friends had been off school for a week and then come back pale and miserable and had never been quite the same again. They'd caught it . . . divorce.

'Upstairs, young lady!' Her mother's voice broke into her thoughts. 'I think you'd better have a bath . . .'

'Not tonight, Mum.'

'Tonight. You've hardly used that bath since it was installed. What's the matter with you? Don't you like it?'

'No. I don't . . .'

That made her father twitch with annoyance. 'What's wrong with it?' he asked, sulking.

But before she could answer, her mother chipped in.

'It doesn't matter what's wrong with it. It's the only bath we've got so you're just going to have to get used to it.'

'I won't.'

Her parents looked at each other, momentarily helpless. Isabel realized that she had never defied them before – not like this. They were thrown. But then her mother stood up. 'Come on, Isabel,' she said. 'I've had enough of this stupidity. I'll come with you.'

And so the two of them went upstairs, Susan with that pinched, set look that meant she couldn't be argued with. But Isabel didn't argue with her. If her mother ran the bath, she would see for herself what was happening. She would see that something was wrong . . .

'Right . . .' Susan pushed the plug in and turned on the taps. Ordinary, hot, clear water gushed out. 'I really don't understand you, Isabel,' she exclaimed over the roar of the water. 'Maybe you've been staying up too late. I thought it was only six-year-olds who didn't like having baths. There!' The bath was full. Susan tested the water, swirling it round with the tips of her fingers. 'Not too hot. Now let's see you get in.'

'Mum . . .'

'You're not shy in front of me, are you? For heavens sake . . .!'

Angry and humiliated, Isabel undressed in front of her mother, letting the clothes fall in a heap on the floor. Susan scooped them up again but said nothing. Isabel hooked one leg over the edge of the bath and let her toes come into contact with the water. It was hot – but not scalding. Certainly not icy cold.

'Is it all right?' her mother asked.

'Yes, Mum . . .'

Isabel got into the bath. The water rose hungrily to greet her. She could feel it close in a perfect circle around her neck. Her mother stood there a moment longer, holding her clothes. 'Can I leave you now?' she asked.

'Yes.' Isabel didn't want to be alone in the bath but she felt uncomfortable lying there with her mother hovering over her.

'Good.' Susan softened for a moment. 'I'll come and kiss you goodnight.' She held the clothes up and wrinkled her nose. 'These had better go in the wash too.'

Susan went.

Isabel lay there on her own in the hot water, trying to relax. But there was a knot in her stomach and her whole body was rigid, shying away from the cast-iron touch of the bath. She heard her mother going back down the stairs. The door of the utility room opened. Isabel turned her head slightly and for the first time caught sight of herself in the mirror. And this time she did scream.

And scream.

In the bath, everything was ordinary, just as her mother had left her. Clear water. Her flesh a little pink in the heat. Steam. But in the mirror, in the reflection . . .

The bathroom was a slaughterhouse. The liquid in the bath was crimson and Isabel was up to her neck in it. As her hand – her reflected hand – recoiled out of the water, the red liquid clung to it, dripping down heavily, splattering against the side of the bath and clinging there too. Isabel tried to lever herself out of the bath but slipped and fell, the water rising over her chin. It touched her lips and she screamed again, certain she would be sucked into it and die. She tore her eyes away from the mirror. Now it was just water. In the mirror . . .

Blood.

She was covered in it, swimming in it. And there was somebody else in the room. Not in the room. In the reflection of the room. A man, tall, in his forties, dressed in some sort of suit, grey face, moustache, small, beady eyes.

'Go away!' Isabel yelled. 'Go away! Go away!'

When her mother found her, curled up on the floor in a huge puddle of water, naked and trembling, she didn't try to explain. She didn't even speak. She allowed herself to be half-carried into bed and hid herself, like a small child, under the duvet.

For the first time, Susan Harding was more worried than annoyed. That night, she sat down with Jeremy and the two of them were closer than they had been for a long time as they talked about their daughter, her behaviour, the need perhaps for some sort of therapy. But they didn't talk about the bath – and why should they? When Susan had burst into the bathroom she had seen nothing wrong with the water, nothing wrong with the mirror, nothing wrong with the bath.

No, they both agreed. There was something wrong with Isabel. It had nothing to do with the bath.

The antique shop stood at the corner of Swiffe Lane and the Fulham Road, a few minutes' walk from the tube station. It was somehow exactly as Isabel had imagined it. From the front it looked like the grand house that might have belonged to a rich family perhaps a hundred years ago: tall imposing doors, shuttered windows, white stone columns and great chunks of statuary scattered between it and the street. But over the years the house had declined, the plaster-work falling away, weeds sprouting between the brick-work. The windows were dark with the dust of city life and car exhaust fumes.

Inside, the rooms were small and dark – each one filled with too much furniture. Isabel and Belinda passed through a room with fourteen fireplaces, an-other with half a dozen dinner tables and a crowd of empty chairs. If they hadn't known all these objects were for sale they could have imagined that the place was still occupied by a rich madman. It was still more of a house than a shop. When the two girls spoke to each other, they did so in whispers.

They eventually found a sales assistant in a courtyard at the back of the house. This was a large, open area, filled with baths and basins, more statues, stone foun-tains, wrought-iron gates and trellis-work – all surrounded by a series of concrete arches that made them feel that they could have been in Rome or Venice rather than a shabby corner of West London. The sales assistant was a young man with a squint and a broken nose. He was carrying a gargoyle. Isabel wasn't sure which of the two was uglier.

'A Victorian bath?' he muttered in response to Isabel's inquiry. 'I don't think I can help you. We sell a lot of old baths.'

'It's big and white,' Isabel said. 'With little legs and gold taps . . .'

The sales assistant set the gargoyle down. It clunked heavily against a paving stone. 'Don't you have the receipt?' he asked.

'No'.

'Well . . . what did you say your parents' name was?'

'Harding. Jeremy and Susan Harding.'

'Doesn't ring a bell . . .'

'They argue a lot. They probably argued about the price.'

A slow smile spread across the sales assistant's face. Because of the way his face twisted, the smile was oddly menacing. 'Yeah. I do remember,' he said. 'It was delivered somewhere in North London.'

'Muswell Hill,' Isabel said.

'That's right.' The smile cut its way over his cheek-bone. 'I do remember. They got the Marlin bath.'

'What's the Marlin bath?' Belinda asked. She didn't like the sound of it already.

The sales assistant chuckled to himself. He pulled

out a packet of ten cigarettes and lit one. It seemed a long time before he spoke again. 'Jacob Marlin. It was his bath. I don't suppose you've ever heard of him.'

'No,' Isabel said, wishing he'd get to the point.

'He was famous in his time.' The sales assistant blew silvery grey smoke into the air. 'Before they hanged him.'

'Why did they hang him?' Isabel asked.

'For murder. He was one of those . . . what do you call them . . . Victorian axe murderers. Oh yes . . .' The sales assistant was grinning from ear to ear now, enjoying himself. 'He used to take young ladies home with him – a bit like Jack the Ripper. Know what I mean? Marlin would do away with them . . .'

'You mean kill them?' Belinda whispered.

'That's exactly what I mean. He'd kill them and then chop them up with an axe. In the bath.' The sales assistant sucked at his cigarette. 'I'm not saying he did it in that bath, mind. But it came out of his house. That's why it was so cheap. I dare say it would have been cheaper still if your mum and dad had known . . .'

Isabel turned and walked out of the antique shop. Belinda followed her. Suddenly the place seemed horrible and menacing, as if every object on display might have some dreadful story attached. Only in the street, surrounded by the noise and colour of the traffic did they stop and speak.

'It's horrible!' Belinda gasped. 'He cut people up in the bath and you . . .' She couldn't finish the sentence. The thought was too ghastly.

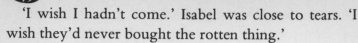

'I wish I hadn't come.' Isabel was close to tears. 'I wish they'd never bought the rotten thing.'

'If you tell them . . .'

'They won't listen to me. They never listen to me.'

'So what are you going to do?' Belinda asked.

Isabel thought for a moment. People pushed past on the pavement. Market vendors shouted out their wares. A pair of policemen stopped briefly to examine some apples. It was a different world to the one she had left behind her in the antique shop. 'I'm going to destroy it,' she said at last. 'It's the only way. I'm going to break it up. And my parents can do whatever they like . . .'

She chose a monkey-wrench from her father's tool-box. It was big and she could use it both to smash and to unscrew. Neither of her parents were at home. They thought she was over at Belinda's. That was good. By the time they got back it would all be over.

There was something very comforting about the tool she had chosen, the coldness of the steel against her palm, the way it weighed so heavily in her hand, almost willing her to swing it. Slowly she climbed the stairs, already imagining what she had to do. Would the monkey-wrench be strong enough to crack the bath? Or would she only disfigure it so badly that her parents would have to get rid of it? It didn't matter either way. She was doing the right thing. That was all she cared.

The bathroom door was open. She was sure it had

been shut when she had glanced upstairs only minutes before. But that didn't matter either. Swinging the monkey-wrench, she went into the bathroom.

The bath was waiting for her.

It had filled itself to the very brim with hot water – scalding hot from the amount of steam it was giving off. The mirror had completely steamed over. A cool breeze from the door touched the surface of the glass and water trickled down. Isabel lifted the monkey-wrench. She was smiling a little cruelly. The one thing the bath couldn't do was move. It could taunt her and frighten her but now it just had to sit there and take what was coming to it.

She reached out with the monkey-wrench and jerked out the plug.

But the water didn't leave the bath. Instead something thick and red oozed out of the plug-hole and floated up through the water.

And with the blood came maggots – hundreds of them, uncoiling themselves from the plug-hole, forcing themselves up through the grille and cartwheeling crazily in the water. Isabel stared in horror, then raised the monkey-wrench. The water, with the blood added to it, was sheeting over the side now, cascading on to the floor. She swung and felt her whole body shake as the metal clanged into the taps, smashing the C of cold and jolting the pipe-work.

She lifted the monkey-wrench and as she did so she caught sight of it in the mirror. The reflection was blurred by the white coating of steam but behind it she could make out another shape which she knew she would not see in the bathroom. A man was walking towards her as if down a long corridor, making for the glass that covered its end. Jacob Marlin. She felt his eyes burning into her and wondered what he would do when he reached the mirror that seemed to be a barrier between his world and hers.

She swung with the monkey-wrench – again and again. The tap bent, then broke off with the second impact. Water spurted out as if in a death-throe. Now she turned her attention on the bath itself, bringing the monkey-wrench crashing into the side, cracking the enamel with one swing, denting the metal with the next. Another glance over her shoulder told her that Marlin was getting closer, pushing his way towards the steam. She could see his teeth, discoloured and sharp, his gums exposed as his lips were drawn back in a rictus of hate. She swung again and saw – to her disbelief – that she had actually cracked the side of the bath like an egg-shell. Red water gushed over her legs and feet. Maggots were sent spinning in a crazy dance across the bathroom floor, sliding into the cracks and wriggling there, helpless. How close was Marlin? Could he pass through the mirror? She lifted the monkey-wrench one last time and screamed as a pair of man's hands fell on her shoulders. The monkey-wrench spun out of her hands and fell into the bath, disappearing in the murky water. The hands were at her throat now, pulling her backwards. Isabel screamed and lashed out, her nails going for the man's eyes.

She only just had time to realize that it was not Marlin who was holding her but her father. That her mother was standing at the door, staring with wide, horror-filled eyes. Isabel felt all the strength rush out of her body like the water out of the bath. The water was transparent again, of course. The maggots had gone. Had they ever been there? Did it matter? She began to laugh.

She was still laughing half an hour later when the sound of sirens filled the room and the ambulance arrived.

It wasn't fair.

Jeremy Harding lay in the bath thinking about the events of the past six weeks. It was hard not to think about them – in here, looking at the dents his daughter had made with the monkey-wrench. The taps had almost been beyond repair. As it was they now dripped all the time and the letter C was gone for ever. Old water, not cold water.

He had seen Isabel a few days before and she had looked a lot better. She still wasn't talking but it would be a long time before that happened, they said. Nobody knew why she had decided to attack the bath – except maybe that fat friend of hers and she was too frightened to say. According to the experts, it had all been stress-related. A traumatic stress disorder. Of course they had fancy words for it. What they meant was that it was her parents' fault. They argued. There was tension in the house. Isabel hadn't been able to cope and had come up with some sort of fantasy related to the bath.

In other words, it was his fault.

But was it? As he lay in the soft, hot water with the smell of pine bath-oil rising up his nostrils, Jeremy Harding thought long and hard. He wasn't the one who started the arguments. It was always Susan. From the day he'd married her, she'd insisted on . . . well, changing him. She was always nagging him. It was like that nickname of his at school. Grumpy. They never took him seriously. She never took him seriously. Well, he would show her.

Lying back with the steam all around him, Jeremy found himself floating away. It was a wonderful feeling. He would start with Susan. Then there were a couple of boys in his French class. And of course, the headmaster.

He knew just what he would do. He had seen it that morning in a junk shop in Crouch End. Victorian, he would have said. Heavy with a smooth wooden handle and a solid, razor-sharp head.

Yes. He would go out and buy it the following morning. It was just what he needed. A good Victorian axe . . .

ACKNOWLEDGEMENTS

The editor and publishers gratefully acknowledge the following for permission to reproduce copyright material in this anthology:

'Secret Terror' from *One Step Beyond* by Pete Johnson, published by Mandarin, copyright © Pete Johnson, 1990, reprinted by kind permission of the author and the Peters Fraser & Dunlop Group Ltd; 'Battleground' from *Night Shift* by Stephen King, copyright © Cavalier, 1972, reprinted by permission of Doubleday, a division of Bantam Doubleday Dell Publishing Group, Inc. and Hodder & Stoughton; 'The Vacancy' from *The Haunting of Chas McGill* by Robert Westall, copyright © Robert Westall, 1983, reprinted by permission of Macmillan Children's Books; 'Freebies' from *Dark Toys and Consumer Goods* by Laurence Staig, copyright © Laurence Staig, 1989, reprinted by permission of Macmillan Children's Books; 'Man from the South' from *Someone Like You* by Roald Dahl, first published in the UK by Secker and Warburg 1954, first published in the US by Alfred A Knopf 1953, copyright © Roald Dahl Nominee Limited, 1948, 1981, 1994, reprinted by permission of Murray Pollinger and the Watkins Loomis Agency; 'The Werewolf Mask' by Kenneth Ireland, first published by Hodder and Stoughton, copyright © Kenneth Ireland, 1983, reprinted by kind permission of the author and the Jennifer Luithlen Agency; 'Eels' from *The Burning Baby and Other Ghosts* by John Gordon, published by Walker Books Ltd, London, copyright © John Gordon, 1992, reprinted by permission of Walker Books Ltd; 'Bath Night' by Anthony Horowitz, copyright © Anthony Horowitz, 1994, reprinted by kind permission of the author.

Every effort has been made to trace copyright holders but in a few cases this has proved impossible. The editor and publishers apologize for these cases of copyright transgression and would like to hear from any copyright holder not acknowledged.